The Vigilante's Diary

Using Fear as a Tool

Jeffrey Berry
of Rawdon Quebec

iUniverse, Inc.
New York   Bloomington

The Vigilante's Diary
Using Fear as a Tool

This is a work of fiction. All of the characters, names, incidents, organizations, and dialogue in this novel are either the products of the author's imagination or are used fictitiously.

iUniverse books may be ordered through booksellers or by contacting:

iUniverse
1663 Liberty Drive
Bloomington, IN 47403
www.iuniverse.com
1-800-Authors (1-800-288-4677)

ISBN: 978-1-4502-4183-0 (dj)
ISBN: 978-1-4502-4184-7 (ebook)

Printed in the United States of America

iUniverse rev. date: 07/16/2010

This is a story about me.

My name is Garrett Berryman and this is my whole life since I was ten years old.

All I ever wanted to do was to be a pro-boxer. I was very good at it, and I knew that's how I would make my living. As I got older, my family was very poor. I knew this was my way out. My father was George Berryman. This man was the best father in the whole world. He would work day and night to make ends meat. With ten kids it was very hard. It didn't matter how hard he tried. He was always in debt. My Mom was a fantastic person and was always feeding other people's kids. She would never see anyone go hungry, even if she had to give up her own supper to give to some kid that had less.

This made me want to turn pro more than ever. I talked to my trainer James Hendrex, who was a pro-boxer, himself. He kept telling me to stay in school, and when I get older we'll talk about it. School was not an important part of my life. At that time I was always in trouble. I had a form of Dyslexia. Back then you were considered stupid or lazy; it's not like today. I was neither. At the age of sixteen I left school to help my parents. I worked at a drug store. I had no time for friends, only working and boxing.

I would give my pay to my Mom to help out. My tips I would use for bus fare to get to the gym. Sometimes I would give Mom my tips too. I would then run the 10 miles. I figured it would be part of my training. My Dad was suffering from ulcers. This was always on my mind; it made me want to turn pro all the more. But there was that word again "WAIT". My trainer kept telling me I have lots of time. I was very impatient, so I went to another gym to do what I had to do. James was very upset and was trying to warn me that this is not the way to go. He would tell me to listen to him, and that this was a dirty game and I was not ready yet. Of course I didn't listen. I would yell at him "you're just jealous that I have a chance to do something with my life and your all washed up".

He kept coming by my house and telling my Dad "tell Garrett to listen to me, but my father would not stand in my way. He always gave me a lot of support. He would come to all of my fights, but as time went on there was no one left to fight in the amateur ranks. I was training furiously, then came my big break. Everyone in the gym knew that I wanted to turn pro, but I would not cross James, because he was well known in the boxing world. James knew deep down that's what I wanted. He was concerned because he knew it was a dirty game and that I was there to win. I wanted to be someone that people would remember {a champion} which I was already. I just had to prove it. So within a couple of weeks after bugging the shit out of the trainer of the current champ, he said to me" you get your chance, you will go five rounds with the champ's sparing partner just to see what you really have. Then we will know where to put you in the ranks and set up your next fight, so be there at 4:00 Monday.

Monday came around and I was in the best shape of my fighting career. The guy I was going to fight was at least twice my weight. I was not worried; when the time came I had a big surprise. The champ himself decided he would get in with me. His trainer was trying to talk him out of it but {he was the champ} so after some arguing the bell rang. He was the showboat. He urged me on and dropping his hands, but he had no clue who I was or what my hands were made of. 30 seconds into the fight I landed a left right to his gut, then a left to his head. It was like a dream. Everything went into slow motion as his head almost got ripped right off. His feet seemed to lift almost waist high, then he hit the ring floor with a thud, he was out cold. The gym just erupted with screams. The ring filled with everyone who was anyone, they were grabbing at me and pulling. I could hear trainer's voices saying" hurry come with me" the voices were coming from all directions. I quickly left the ring to go and change with a big crowd following me. I was scared and happy at the same time, but all these guys that wouldn't have anything to do with me before were trying to get me to sign with them all at once. I said I'll be back tomorrow then I left. I was singing and laughing and making plans with all the money I was going to make. After celebrating with a few beers I drove home with my drinking buddy Kent. As we sat in my van talking and reflecting on the night." I said lets go up stairs" as I started to open my door to the van, I could see headlights in my side mirror. I waited for the car to pass before I got out but it didn't, so I decided to get out. Kent was already walking towards the back of the van, as I turned to get out I heard aloud bang with a flash, then the car that was behind me suddenly tore by me. I could see three black guys in the car. One guy was pulling in a long gun, and then I heard Kent scream"Garrette are you o.k." I was confused but I answered" what was that? Kent was yelling they shot you man. I guess I was in shock because I didn't feel anything at first, then I looked down and my left leg. It was just hanging there. I tried to lift it in the van but it was so heavy it felt like it weighed a ton. I didn't know what to make of it. Who would do this? Then the police came. I was sitting there; the pain was a hot throbbing terrible pain. The cops were asking who would do this. I was as confused as could be. I told them what I seen and then two or three other cop cars went looking for them. As they were transporting me to the Hospital the cops were asking me where I was last, so I told them about the fight.

The next day I awoke and suddenly remembered what happened, I panicked, and then yelled for the nurse. To my surprise there was a cop watching the door to my room and would not let anyone in. I was under police protection. I got more and more confused. After the nurse gave me something for the pain. I went back to sleep, when I woke up, there was two cops waiting to talk to me. How do you feel? They asked, I said this must be a bad dream, the cop said no sir this is no dream, we checked out your story about the fight with the champ, but nobody seen or heard of you, that's not unusual, the gym that you talked about and the people you spoke of, are not very nice. We have been looking into this bunch for a long time for different criminal acts. It is a branch of the Mob so they will not talk, I replied! The gym was full someone had to see me. They were all trying to get me to sign with them.

The gym was full, I'm sorry sir, and after your release we want you to come down town to look at some photos. All this was too much for me, the Doctor came in after the cops left and hit me with the bad news, that I was hit with a 12 gauge shot gun. With the amount of lead in your leg I figure two barrels plus they put glass and rags inside, they didn't want you to box again. I was very depressed my life was flashing before my eyes what was I going to do? I dropped out of school and quit my job. My parents were terrified that I was going to be killed. Nothing like this has ever happened to my family. I felt bad not for me but for my parents. I felt like I let them down, I wanted to Box so bad, and I knew that was my way out of poverty.

My Dad got sick, and then I turned to the bottle. My whole life was a mess. Then my Dad said to me one day that in the Bible it said" nothing is impossible" you have to believe that, but I was in a bad depression, unable to work. I was on Welfare for a long time trying to get back on my feet. My leg was not much good. So after about five years the Doctor's decided to amputate. Not long after that my Dad passed away. My whole family just seemed to fall apart. I felt like it was my entire fault. My Mom was a real mess after that. It got worse I turned to heavy drugs Cocaine & Crack, I was stealing. I felt like there was no hope. At one point I wanted to die, would take such big hits of Cocaine that I would pass out.

Then I started to look at my life one day when I was visiting my Father's grave, I started to cry uncontrollably, apologizing to my Dad for the mess that I had made.

Then I started to pray, I never prayed unless I needed something, this time my prayers were real, not because I needed food or money, but for forgiveness for all my sins. I sat there by my Father's grave crying and praying in the pouring rain, I said" please my God help me help myself to stop the drugs and the drinking and to make something of my life". I always believed in God but this day was the beginning of my new life.

After I got home I dumped out all the beer, tossed out the crack pipe, then I spoke to my brother about living in his Country place. He agreed. Already the Lord was working with me. I hit bottom and now it was time to reflect.

I lived the first year in the Country with no running water and no toilet, but I was never so happy. After I stopped drinking and doing drugs all my so called" friends" never even returned a phone call. It was not me they liked; it was what I stood for. With all the drugs and the booze out of my life, all the people I called" friends" couldn't care less. Why should they talk to me when I wasn't the same guy? I finally realized it wasn't me they liked it was the bottle or the drugs. Now it was my time to move ahead with my life. It came to a point where I would sit there in the dark of the woods sober for the first time in eight years and thank God for saving me and my family. No one that I knew, where I was living, drank or did drugs, but it was very visible around me, Bikers ran the town that I moved to. The only jobs in town was growing weed or selling it, but I wouldn't have anything to do with it. I wanted to be honest. I was doing handy crafts but barely making a living. If I made $60.00 a month it was good. It was heart-breaking to see all these dirt bags getting ahead while my wife and I were having such a hard time, but my faith is strong, and the more I prayed the better things got for us.

One day I was in the Village selling my crafts, I was approached by a small thin man that I seen around before, he was a Notary, he seemed very nice. He bought everything I had and made orders for more. I was blessed again. As I got to know him a little better he made me an offer," How would you like to make some good money? Maybe twenty Thousand dollars, all you have to do is water some pot plants once a week." I said,

"No way, I have been clean for some time and I want to keep it that way." he said there's no risk, your a nice guy and I want to help you do this and by the end of the year you'll be a rich guy. If anything happens, if the cops catch you it will only be a fine that's it and I'll pay everything. It was to good for me to pass up, so I agreed.

I kept convincing myself that it was just this one time. All I wanted to do was get ahead. That was my biggest mistake, trusting someone with that much money. I grew the weed for him but when it was time to harvest; the cops raided the field and caught me. I knew better than to say anything so I took the rap. When I got out of jail, three days later I called him to pay the thousand-dollar fine. He played like he knew nothing about it. I was fucked.

That's when it happened; I decided to become a vigilantly. I knew then I had to do something. The worse thing was he worked for the bikers. I sat back for about a year, and apologized to God and to my Father for being stupid. I swore from that day forward I would fight crime. I didn't want anyone else to fall for the bullshit that I fell for. They pray on the poor and the weak

Knowing that money is the key to make the weak even weaker. But I will not stand by and watch them destroy lives anymore.

My story of revenge starts here 10 years to the day of my

shooting Oct 1991. The bikers were in charge of everything. Starting with the police

{Being hopeless and helpless all at the same time}, they took over Bars, Homes, and Farmer's field's etc.... Everyone was scared of these guys,

Why? I kept asking myself, just numbers. By themselves they were no bigger or better than anyone else, only when there was a gang of them, "safety in numbers they say". I was just one man out to make a difference, but I kept thinking, how? There must be a way. I started watching the small Bars in town where I knew the bikers were selling drugs. It use to be a nice place all the old timers would go and reminisce about old times, {it use to be fun to see} until the bikers stole it from the owner. I watched this place go from a fun place to sit and talk, to a drug Den where the dope heads would just go to buy drugs. The Police knew but did nothing. The owner of the Bar was old and scared. These guys just came in and took over. They would drink for free and take money from the till. It was disgusting to see, but I stayed there and watched. There were four guys that would go there on a regular week, changing days. They were members of the Devils Guards, mostly yellow when they were alone. I know this because one night as I sat there, some guy who was just passing through for a beer with his girl friend, this biker approached him trying to sell him drugs. The guy stood up and said no thanks I don't do drugs.

The Biker kept insisting" come on" the guy stood up again, this time he was mad."fuck off or I'll call the cops" He didn't know that this guy was a member of a gang, the Biker said" o.k. man, don't take a fit, I was just trying to make a sale," then he went to the back {the Biker} of the Bar and made a phone call.

The stranger sat back down and was very proud of himself, he told his girl friend to finish her beer then we'll leave. Within minutes there were three other Bikers coming in the back door all showing their colors and talking to

the other Biker, then you could see them talking about this poor guy. He was scared and told his girl-friend to leave and go wait in the car, she was clearly upset and was hesitant to leave, but just after she went out the door

two of the Bikers went out the back the other two started towards him, he tried to get out as fast as he could, but before he could move ten feet, the two Bikers jumped him and started to beat on this guy, he was yelling for someone to call the police but everyone in the Bar knew better. The owner tried to stop them but he got a beating also. By this time I had seen enough, after the guy left bleeding and his girlfriend with big red marks on her face, I was really upset to say the least, but I kept my cool and sat there until they all started laughing and making fun of this poor guy, then I got up to leave and this Biker that started the whole thing walked up to me and said" did you see that?" I replied "see what" and he just turned around walked away laughing. They were very proud of themselves, it was disgusting, but at that moment my fear became anger and that's when I made my move. I went home and started to make a plan, I knew as long as I told no one, no one would know. I took my .22 and loaded it. 14 shots, each bullet was sanded to a point and then sprayed with Teflon for maximum penetration.

I was ready to start my new job, but I had to be very careful not to be seen. I was declaring war on the Bikers and they had no clue what was about to happen. I went back to the Bar just like I have been doing for weeks, but this time it was different. I parked my Jimmy in another parking lot about 300 Feet away and I just sat there waiting for this little prick and his gang of tough guys. I knew that on Wednesdays they would all be together in the Bar. My .22 had a home made silencer, made from a plastic bottle taped with black tape so there wouldn't be a flash. When the first biker came out I waited for him to get close to his car, just as he opened his door I fired two shots BANG, BANG he fell to the ground I quickly stuck another piece of tape over the hole in the bottle to get ready for my next shot. Then minutes later two more came out, they noticed that the other biker's car was still there so they both walked towards the car as they got closer I took aim, then I could see that one guy started back towards the bar BANG. He fell face first, there was no noise, the other guy spotted his friend and started to run for his car, he was

shitting himself trying to get the keys out of his pocket, then I fired BANG, BANG there was one more, the one I wanted the most, now I have three dead bikers in the parking lot, but I knew no one would even notice because no one went out back,{out of fear of these guys}, then the little prick came out, when he seen one guy lying on the ground he said joking "What's up man are you sick" then he turned the guy over he sprang back just like someone kicked him, he started to run but was so scared he couldn't stay on his feet, he kept falling, then I fired BANG, BANG every shot hitting it's target l in the head. Then I packed up and went home, saying nothing; my wife asked" me where are you working?" I gave her some fake name, she never questioned me after that, but I told her that I'll be working some strange hours from now on because the people work shift work, and I could only work when they are there. Later on that night I could hear the police cars going to the bar from my house, the hair stood up on the back of my neck, but I tried not to think of it. I knew why they were going there, but my silence is part of the job and long as I thought of this as a job, I was O.K., it bothered me that I just killed four guys, but I felt justified. It was the lesser of two evils. I just hope God can forgive me, but I won't know that until we meet.

The next day it was all over town, the Nasty Ones killed four of the Devils Guards right outside the Bar, the police and the papers thought the same thing, it was a settling of accounts, then with no help from me the Devils Guards shot two of the Nasty Ones, this went on for a day or two, the war was on. There were cars being blown up and Bikers killing each other left and right. So now it was my move. I went to a Bar in another town where the Nasty Ones had control, this time there was one guy, a big fat pig that was selling drugs to students, but he wasn't that easy to get to, this gave me the shakes, but it was just another job, but this time I made a blow gun it was about four feet long, the dart was made of paper with a knitting needle about 6 inches long, then I just waited for him outside the Bar. He was in and out a few times, but always with someone, then about an hour later he came out with a young girl about 17years old and was fooling around with her, then they started walking towards the car. He sat in the front seat with the door opened, his two feet on the ground he was telling the young girl to give him "head", she got down on her knees and started to blow him and that's when I took my shot. I took a deep breath then I fired, the dart got him right into the right eye, he fell back in his seat clutching the girl's head so tight that she couldn't move. He was just lying there shaking just like someone having a seizure. The girl jumped up after he let go, she started screaming and yelling than started to run into the bar. As soon as she was gone, so was I. As I was on my way back home the police were coming from everywhere. Within minutes, my heart was pounding so hard I thought I was going to have a heart attack. I could feel it coming right through my chest; this was not a good feeling. Then I looked out my rear view mirror and seen two or three police cars speeding towards me with flashers on and sirens going. I was a mess. I was shaking and sweating. I was sure my heart was going to pop, then they passed, I was never so relieved in my life. I pulled over to the side of the road got out and pissed, which seemed like forever, then I seen the ambulance coming and right after that two or three bikers speeding after it. Now I was shitting, what did I start? I had to keep telling myself that I was doing well but deep down I knew it was murder. It was to late to start doubting my work. The guy I just killed was a drug dealer and a pimp, not just a pimp but was pimping kids. Getting them hooked on drugs, some of the kids were no more than thirteen or fourteen years old. I have family that age, it's a terrible thing to see kids so young doing coke, their lives are over once they start at that age.

The last few days were very uneasy for me. I could not shake that image of the guy they called little Joe, his body lying there shaking like that, but he had it coming. For days after, the newspapers couldn't get enough of the violence. It was front-page news every time one of these guys died. Then I saw a picture of Little Joe in the French paper that showed police photos of his body on the table of the morgue, my dart firmly sticking out of his eye. His body covered in Tattoos. It made me sick; I went into the bathroom and was pucking my guts up. My wife kept asking," Are you o.k.?"

"No" I replied," I must have eaten something." The sight of a body that closes scared me to no end. I was making progress, every time I killed one, the other gang would kill another member of the other gang. They were killing each other for weeks. The cops kept saying "settling of accounts" they never even bothered to look for a suspect. They could care less, there was no innocent people getting hurt. So they just kept on counting the dead.

The news always had headlines I thought this was a good thing at first, but the Bikers started to talk among themselves. That's when they knew it had to be someone else. I had to let things die down a bit before my next job. Then on the news they aired a story that the Devil's Guards and the Nasty Ones will become one gang and join forces. They lost a lot of men during this war and they started picking on the little gangs like the Voodoo Kings, a Haitian gang that ran the east end, they killed 12 members at a Bar. They just walked in and shot up the place with

Machine guns, but that did not go unpunished. The Kings caught two members of the Nasty Ones eating lunch, and chopped them to death with masheti's, these guys like knives not guns, but were no match for The Devils Guards. There was just too many of them along with the Nasty Ones, they killed most of them by drive-by's and firebombs. It did not take long; there were no more Kings. They were killing all the little guys that they thought had something to do with the killings but. I told no one so no one knew it was me. Now I had to start all over because they were right back doing the same shit in the same Bars. The cops couldn't care less now. It was making me mad, I did not like killing these guys but I was driven by a force that I could not explain. Now I was in it for the long run. I was fucked no matter how I looked at it; if the cops catch me it's life in jail. If the Bikers catch me I am dead, and I still have to answer to God when the time comes. I told my wife I had a big job to do, and I would be gone for a few days. I did not know what I was going to do, but I left in my Jimmy with my.22, then I started to read the French papers to keep up on the Bikers activity's and sure enough they had a two page spread on a large rally that was going to take place in Quebec city. They were coming from all over, hundreds of them. In the states, they could care less of the cops, because the cops could do nothing they had bunkers surrounded by sand bags. They had armed lookouts. It was a fortress. The cops just stood by and took photos. I made other plans. This was my chance to strike fear into these guys the same way they put fear into the public.

I found a nice spot to hide in a farmer's field about 200 feet away from the highway where they had to pass to get to the Club

House where the meeting was going to take place. I laid there for hours just waiting for them to pass, and then just as I started to fall asleep I could hear the rumble of hundreds of bikes in the distance. I could see them coming two by two, that's all you could see for about two miles. This put a fear in me so bad that I was shaking uncontrollably, but I was there and there was no changing the plan at this point. I could see them clearly, both gangs riding with full colors. It was sickening to see flaunt the law, but I had to concentrate about business at hand. I knew that the first six or eight were just scouts, speeding ahead to check out what was ahead, but my shots were not to be wasted. I had fourteen, all sharpened and sprayed with Teflon. I was ready as I would ever be. As soon as

I got the first two bikers in my sight I waited until there were ten or twelve together then I fired, making every shot count the first two I fired bang, bang, the 22. Went right through the helmets of the first two bikers, they left the road

Crashing and flipping. Then I kept firing bang, bang, bang, the bikers were falling all over each other. It looked like something out of a movie. It was just carnage; out of the fourteen shots I hit fourteen. I killed and manned over twenty-five. The rest of the bikers were slamming on brakes and spinning out. It was amazing to see, everything seemed to happen in slow motion. They were all going in different directions lacing their buddy's all over the road and in ditches. Some were going so fast that they were running into each other. They had no idea who was shooting at them or from where. It was a real sight. The traffic that was on the road was also killing them. This was a major highway. Within minutes I could hear the police and the fire dept coming so I got out of there. It wasn't hard; everyone was coming to see the crash. I walked back to my truck and went home. That night the six o'clock news had a live and full coverage of this breaking story. Every channel was running it for days. Then the police held a press conference to say that they had fourteen bikers shot dead and over twenty-five more that were in serious condition.

The Bikers were scared to leave their homes, and were turning themselves in to the police. All the bikers' activity stopped, they were terrified to do any business at all, half of them were in jail and the rest were hiding. This was a good sign, or was it? Now the police started a new course of action: Find out who's doing the killing of the Bikers. They had a press conference asking for help from the public. The Bikers that struck fear into so many people for so long were now scared and paranoid. They didn't trust anyone not even their own. They were killing snitches and prostitutes and cops that were on the take. They were found dead and raped and were shot several times, and put in sleeping bags for the police to find. After this the cops started to look in their own backyards for brothers that were let go for excessive force, or taking the law into their own hands by beating criminals and was suspended.

I waited and watched for weeks as the Bikers went from a large force of feared thugs, to a gang of scared rabbits, looking for help from the cops, telling them that it wasn't them that were doing the killing. It was an outside force. The cops agreed, now I had to be very careful, it was not just the bikers that were looking for this killer or killers so were the cops. This would make my new job more dangerous than ever, but I believe that as long as I don't say anything about my job, no one will ever know it's me.

After my last killing it seemed to get easier. It's like I lost part of my soul, and taking a life was just another job. This made it easier to continue. Now I had them on the run it was time to go after the big- shots, but they were in hiding. Some of the little fish were still bringing them money and dope, so I hit all the coke dealers in town one at a time. As I started to watch these guys, there were a lot of unexpected people involved like natives from two different reserves that could come and go freely over the borders without much trouble. How will I stop this flow of drugs without being seen, or worse, caught? If they catch me I am dead. If the cops catch me I'll go to jail with all my new friends, that's not much of a choice! I had to think very hard of my next move. I can't wait to long, the longer I wait the more drug money they make. So I made a vow to get rid of all the small dealers and scumbags, or as many as I could anyway without drawing too much attention to the cops. My first thought was no "body" no crime. I started with a local drug dealer that was dealing for the bikers, he was a real asshole, he would sell to anyone at any age, so I watched him for a day or two and I noticed that he would always close the bar and leave drunk and walk home. I used this. On the next night I waited for him, it was about two in the morning he left the bar drunk, as I expected I waited for just the right moment, then I pulled up and offered him a ride, of course he jumped at the chance, as he got into my truck I smashed him with a right across the head, he went out cold, now what to do with him? I took him to a place in the woods not far from where I lived. It belonged to a farmer friend of mine; he owned about one hundred acres of land. He was very old and I did a lot of work for him in the past, and I knew the property well so it was safe, he never checked his land, he left that to me. It was one of my jobs that I kept regularly. Getting to my point of origin, I took the drunk out of the truck and laid him next to a pile of wood chips, then I went to the back of my truck to get a knife, as I got to his sleeping body I was just about to slice his throat when he woke up with a start, it scared me, I jumped back in surprise, he started to yell and scream, "help me, help me please", he was still drunk and very unstable on his feet but tried to run anyway falling and screaming as I chased him through the dark woods, he kept yelling" who are you ?,what did I do?", at this point he was in tears and begging for his life as he tried furiously to get away from me, I just kept walking as fast as I could towards him as he was crawling on his belly screaming for help, then I jumped on him with my fish knife, he just kept trying to stop me by grabbing at the knife, but I just kept stabbing at him, hitting him in hands and arms at first, then I struck him in the face with my free hand, by this time I think I was more scared than he was, I kept

Sticking with the knife, but he refused to die. I must have stabbed him more than a dozen times when his body went limp and there was a gurgling sound, then he finally died. I sat there covered in blood and out of breath and panting very heavily, this was a very bad experience for me, it was the first time I killed someone so close. After sitting there for awhile to catch my breath, I had to get rid of this body, so I dug a big hole and placed him inside, I knew that no one would find him there.

The next day I went back to the farm and had a talk with the old man, I went on to ask him if there was anything that I could do for him. I already knew the answer, he replied yes and gave me a list of things to do, and this was a good thing, I told him I would come every day or every second day just to take care of things for him and that he did not have to worry about anything. He was not well so agreed quickly. I went on to tell him that I would come at different hours because of other work. Now I was in business, I could come and go as I pleased and I could continue with my work undisturbed. Just his customers and his biker boss and his old lady, who was hooked on crack, did not miss the guy I killed at all. After a day or two the biker, who was supplying him, came to collect his money, but got a shock when the crack head couldn't tell him anything. He went on to beat her, but she knew nothing and the more she denied it, the angrier he became. He kept hitting her, and saying I want my fucking money, But she was clueless, then he said" I'll be back tomorrow," so I had to work fast. The first thing I had to think about was that he was never alone when he came to collect, thanks to my handy work in the passed. I left a small note on her door pretending to be her old man: I spent their money, but I'll pay it back, but for now I'll stay with my friend until I get the money, I am at 3939Apple Drive. I knew that when the biker showed up, she would give up the information to him for a hit of crack, and she did just what I suspected.

The house was the home of a retired man who was gone to Florida. I took care of his home for the past five years, so I knew it well. Within twenty-four hours he came to the house with his friend and was banging at the door, but I sat there very quietly watching his every move. He kept trying the doors and yelling, "I know your in there let me in so we could talk", all I want is my money, so I did just that, I turned the lock hard enough for him to hear it open, then he told his buddies to go around the back incase he bolts. He entered the house then started going from room to room, I could hear him "where are you." I sat quietly waiting for him to get closer, then he said" stop this bullshit and come out, I promise I won't hurt you, all I want is my money." As he entered the room where I was hiding I had the same fear consume me, and I started to shake just like the first time. Then he called out to his buddy "did you see him",

" No" he replied. As the boss turned to leave the room I jumped up and stuck him right in the throat with my fish knife, he could not scream but was gasping like crazy through the hole in his throat the blood was pissing out just like a water gun, he kept grabbing at my arms as I tried to stick him again, then he fell to the ground, dying, that same sound left his body, it was a gurgling sound I knew then that it was over. Then I heard his buddy coming in the house and was calling "where are you?" my heart was a mess, it was doing back flips and it was pumping so hard I could hear it in my head.

The Boss was lying on the floor half dead and too weak to move, but his buddy was getting closer by the moment and yelling, "where the fuck are you? Stop fucking around," then I heard this buddy chambering around with a semi-automatic hand gun, the sound is unmistakable, so I had to think fast, so I started to scream "please don't kill me, I have your money" then the other guy ran into the room looking to find his boss lying there in a pool of blood, as he turned to run he was yelling," Oh Fuck, Oh Fuck," I slammed the door shut, then began to slash at him, hitting him, the gun hand first. After the gun fell to the floor with his hand still attached, the gun was firing on it's own, he was trying to open the door with his severed hand, but I just grabbed him and cut his throat. Now I had two more bodies to get rid of and a very big mess to clean up. I put both bodies in the trunk of their car and drove them to the farm where I had to find a better way to get rid of the bodies, then I remembered the farmer putting a dead goat in the wood chipper and he went on to tell me that was the best way to get rid of dead animals, because it would break down faster than if he had to bury it. He would then mix it in with the wood chips, and soon after it would become food for the bugs. So I took one body out, took off his clothes and jewelry the stuck him in very large wood chipper feet first, he got sucked in so fast that it was just incredible he came out the other side just like wood chips, so I did the same to the other guy, than I ran some big branches through the chipper to cover it up. Then I took the car to the airport and left it here. Now I had to go back to the house and clean up. After I cleaned up, I went back home. My wife was getting suspicious and asking questions," your doing all this work and I don't see any money," I joked and said,

"Well I can't have money and do drugs to. She replied

" Very funny," then I told her I was not finished, but I'll get some money soon. The truth was I was getting careless and had to be more careful because my new job was becoming an obsession and money never even crossed my mind, and if I was not more careful I could start to neglect the most important things in my life. I did not want that, my family is what I live for, without them I would have nothing. So I went back to the farm where I buried the clothes from the last two guys, and took the money from their pockets so that I could stay home for a while and put my wife's mind at ease.

I continued to do work at the farm for a day or two, catching up on some of the work, getting ahead, this would make the farmer very happy because this was less for him to worry about, knowing that the work was done and he could depend on me, and the wife was happy that I made a few bucks and that I was helping the farmer. He was always very good to us, plus I needed that farm for my other job.

My next order of business was to stop the importers of the drugs, but before I had a chance to plan my next job the farmer called and asked me to come down, he needed to talk t, at least three o me, it was very important. I started to panic, going over all the shit in my mind that I have being down at the farm; My first thought was he found something! I was reliving every moment in my head, maybe he found blood, and maybe he found pieces of flesh. There was a lot of maybe's. There was only one way to find out, so I left to go down to the farm to see him. My mind was a total mess, as I got closer to the farm. I saw at least three police cars, all sitting there with their flashers going and about six cops milling about. I was now shitting myself; my heart was pounding so hard I swear it was going to pop right out of my chest. My mouth was dry to the point that I felt like I just ate a cup of flour. My first thought was to run, but I kept talking myself down from this paranoid feeling, and I tried not to panic, as I got closer. I kept thinking of alibi and answers to questions that no one even asked yet. I was a real bag of nerves, as I got closer and pulled into his driveway and stopped the truck. Two cops started to walk towards me, I was shaking like crazy then the cops said to me, "Who are you?" I was never so relieved in my life to hear those words, then before I had a chance to say anything, I seen two cars all smashed up and a dead cow, I was so happy to give my name. Just then the farmer came out yelling, "it's o.k, he works for me."Shit what a relief, then the farmer went on to tell me why he called, we had to get rid of the cow it was in very bad shape that way it would not be eaten. So I took the backhoe and buried it. When I did that I took all the waste from the last two guys from the wood chipper and put everything in the same hole. After I was finished I went back to tell him that I was done, he invited me in for a tea, then we started to talk about the accident then he said" be careful when you are working out there in the fields my friend." three farms up, the bikers put weed in his field and told

him if he tried to stop them in anyway, his family would pay with their lives.

He did not know it but he just gave me another job, but there was no hurry if they were growers they would be there all summer, so I had a lot of time to plan for this job, I will just wait for the right time.

Meanwhile I went out to find another pusher. It was more

difficult, but not impossible with the other guys gone. With no signs of violence even the cops were starting to ask questions around bars, so I was more careful than usual.

My next job was a guy who was dealing dope in town for along time, but the cops seem to ignore him, that just made it more suspicious of him and the police. It turns out that I was right, after watching this guy for about a week I seen his supplier dropping off a package, the thing that bothered me most was that I knew this guy, but I couldn't place his face, with all the other bikers that bothered me. Where do I know him? I kept asking myself, he was just another biker, and went on with my job. This pusher hardly left his house so I had to get him on his turf, so I took an old vcr removed the guts and replaced them with a very large pipe bomb hooked up to an old switch. All he had to do was plug it in and turn it on, but how do I get him to take the VCR? It was easier than I expected, I just left it outside his door after he went to sleep, with a note that said take this until I can pay you back the money I owe you, and I signed it j.c.

The next day around ten o'clock at night I heard the blast, it was huge, I lived over three miles away and my house shook. My wife jumped up and went running outside with me right behind her, she was saying what was that? I said I don't know, but I'm going to find out. Not long after the blast we could hear the fire trucks and the police going to the scene, I told my wife I would be right back I just want to see what happened, and if anyone was hurt. I jumped in my truck and went to the scene, when I got there I was shocked of the amount of damage that I have done. The whole front of the house was gone, there were bricks and broken glass everywhere, you could see the inside of the house beside it. It was bigger than what I needed, but one thing for sure he was dead, and the police would be lucky if they find his body in one piece.

The real shock was when I saw his supplier sitting there in a unmarked police car, he was a cop not just a cop, a bad cop! What do I do now? I went home and told my wife it must have been a gas leak because the house was finished, I don't know if anyone was hurt but we'll probably hear something on the news later.

I started to make a plan for my next job, but now things have changed, there was a crooked cop and if there's one there's two or more. This raises a lot of questions like; does he work for the bikers? Or is he just a scumbag or both? I'll make it my business to find out. My first guess was right, he worked for the bikers that's how they got all their inside information and it would explain why the bikers got away with so much shit. I was not going to let this little prick get away with anything, in my mind he was just another biker, he had a badge and I had the advantage, now I know him and what he stands for, he has know clue that I know who he is and what he is, and he doesn't know who I am. What do I do, kill a cop or call a cop? I don't think I'll call a cop, but the question is how many are involved? This is getting more complicated and more dangerous by the day. If I stop now they'll win and I don't like to lose. I guess he as to be my next job. How do you kill a cop? It's not like killing a biker, where no one cares if the bikes die only other bikers, but a cop, that's different all together. If I just kill him he'll most likely become a hero, and I don't want that, but if I watch him he could help me. I did just that and now he will work for me and not even know it. I will follow him around and when ever I could. It didn't take very long to see that this scum bag was a gold mine for me and would lead me to some very big fish, including more cops and lawyers, and members of the community that were very rich. I would have never thought that they would be involved, if I hadn't seen it for myself.

I decided to shake the money tree and see what fell out. So to start my first move was to let the rich guy know that I knew he was involved with the bikers and crooked cops. So I paid a visit to his home. It was a very large house on the Lake Shore, I went there to do some surveillance and believe me, money doesn't make you smart. This guy was a real prince. He owned an Old Age home that was passed down from his Father. This guy never did a hard days work in his life, but thought he was above the Law because of his connections and money. In most case he was. He could afford the best lawyers or call the right cop, or just tell bikers of his problem and they would take care of it for a price. The worse thing was that if I tried to expose him no one would believe me because of his position in the community.

I watched his place for a few days. He had a regular schedule that he kept and his house was full of alarms. It would be very hard to go inside. I learned along time ago that people with money don't like to spend it, that's why they have so much and I will use that to enter the house. Every time he would leave his home to go to the hospital for work I waited about twenty minutes, then I shook his front door, to set off the alarm, soon after the regular cops would come, he would show up, they would look around and then leave. I did this every day, watching his house. Then on the third day the cops told him the next time there's a false alarm he would pay a fine. He was very upset about this. The next day the alarm company came and looked around then left. So the very next day I did the same thing. I went over and shook the door then I left and watched from a distance. The cops came first then he showed up about ten minutes later. The police were upset and said they have better things to do and gave him a fine. This got him very angry, and to make things worse they warned him, the next time the fine would be double." That's it! he said," I'll leave it off until I find out what's causing the problem."

I started work the next day. The minute he left I went inside by the back door and waited in the closet in his bedroom. I waited about two hours when I heard his car pull up beside the house, that's when I went into action. This was my chance to get some answers. I knew he could help me with my job. As he entered the bedroom I watched him through a crack in the half open closet door. He took off his pants and laid them on the bed, and then he came right for the closet where I was waiting for him with a wire coat hanger. When he opened that door I let out such a scream, he jumped back screaming and the more I screamed the more he screamed, then in his state of fear he was trying to get away from me, he was so scared that he shit himself. It was all over and making it impossible for him to stand. I started to whip him with the coat hanger, he was freaking out and kept screaming and yelling," what do you want?" but I would not answer him, until I knew he was ready to talk. After whipping him a few more times across the legs, he passed out. He was full of blood and shit. After I woke him up he was willing to tell me anything, and he did. He gave me names of other cops plus he told me where he kept the money. I told him I didn't come here for the money. When I said that his face got red and he started to beg for his life, he said he'd do anything I wanted. I replied," yes you will if you want to live."

he knew when I didn't want money I meant business, so I went on to tell him call your cop friend detective Pattree and tell him what ever you have to, to get him here. Tell him to come at 9:00 tonight and if your convincing enough I'll let you live. He was scared to death, but happy to comply. After he made the call I tied him up then took my fish knife out of its case. Then he started to panic screaming," please don't kill me" I just looked at him and said," do you know how many people that you already killed with the drugs, the bad cops and the Bikers", then I said explain it to God when you meet him.

I won't forgive you, but he might. Then I took my knife and stuck it at the base of his skull and scrambled his brains. After he died I put his body in the lake with an anchor from his boat. I waited for the cop and his 9:00 am appointment, meanwhile I had some time to kill so I started to look around this very big house, then I seen the freezer, I had no idea what I was about to find. I figured out there was some cash from his confession earlier; I was un-prepared for what I found. The freezer was full! It was packed tight, right to the top with large bills, I was shocked I never seen so much money. I just wanted to grab all the money and leave but I knew that if I did, that all my work would be for nothing. So I talked myself out of it and waited for the 9:00 am appointment because something's was more important then money and this was one of them. After a few deep breaths and some deep thought I waited in anticipation for the cop to show up. I had two hours to kill before he got there and it seemed like it took forever. I could not get the money off my mind, I just kept saying to myself "stick to the plan" then before I knew it I heard his car pull up beside the house, this is it a cop I said to myself as he walked around to come in the opened door, he had no clue what was about to happen. He entered the house with a bottle of wine in his hand yelling "hello." As he entered I came from behind the door and struck him on the head with a large piece of art and he quickly fell to the floor. I took his gun and used his handcuffs to restrain him to the bed, when he came through. He was very confused and bleeding and kept asking what happened? What's going on? Who are you? And where is Paul? I said Paul is resting. Now I need some things from you, and if you don't give me what I want I will kill you. He kept saying I'm a cop; you're making a big mistake. I said,

" There's no mistake I know everything, but your going to give me more. I need addresses of all the other assholes that you work for. The head guys of both gangs." He kept saying,

"You don't understand I'm a cop." I just said

" I know everything and being a bad cop won't help you." Then I took a pillow, put the gun inside and shot him in the knee." Now, I will ask you again, names and addresses, NOW," he gave me just what I wanted; I said" I have a job to do."

I put the gun in the pillow and shot him in the head. I put his body in the trunk of his car and drove it into the Lake. Now how do I move a freezer full of money, and where do I put it? There's a lot of money there, and it would put a big dent in the bikers' budget if it disappeared. I could not even imagine how much was there. I took about Five hundred thousand out of the freezer and spread the rest of it all over the house, then I took a mix of gas and heating oil poured it all over the house then I lit a smoke and put in a pack of matches like a fuse, and ten minutes later the house was like an inferno. By the time the fire department got there the house was on the ground. And I was rich and full of information. Now where do I put the money I took? I gave some to my wife and told her I got paid. The rest of it I took to the Farm and buried it, everything was working out. The good cops were upset; they were holding news conferences asking for help from the public. {The rich guy's family was baffled}. There was no mention of the missing cop at all; there was no body, so there was no crime.

My next move was to lay low for a while. All this action was taking its toll on me. I had to let things simmer down a bit and see what all my hard work was doing to the bikers, the money was a big blow to them and they still had no clue who was doing all this. They were asking questions but very carefully not to let anyone no that they were even a part of a gang, and since I never said a word to anyone no one knew anything. They were like rabbits out to get what they wanted then run and hide; now I had to deal with the information I got from the cop just before he died. There was the two heads of the biker gangs and their lawyers, and the lawyers were bikers they just had a law degree, so they knew all the in's and out's. The two head bikers were hiding but did not know the cop gave me their whereabouts. I wanted to get the lawyers first because that was the bikers' link to the outside. The prisons were over flowing with these guys, they were safe there, plus they had all the drugs they needed it was like a camp for these guys.

My next job was the lawyers. I had to make it hard for these guys that were on the inside. It was sickening to hear the guys that were inside doing time for fines, telling stories of the bikers shooting up and smoking heroin like it was legal or buying smokes. The first lawyer was a Jewish man in his fifties his name was Josh Freedman, he was well known by everyone who knew anything about the bikers. He was always the one making statements to the press and defending these guys. I'm sure he was well paid. I watched him for a while and he kept in touch constantly with the two head bikers who ran bars and restaurants legally, and if the cop didn't tell me the names and places of these guys I never would have guessed that they were involved with the bikers. They kept a very low profile and were respected by the community as being good businessmen. On one of Mr. Freedman's visits was to a local restaurant for lunch with his bodyguard. I was waiting for him across the road in my truck with my .22,he always sent out his bodyguard first, then I waited, when the guard came out I took aim and timing was everything. The second he stuck his head in view I fired two shots bang, bang. Freedman fell. The bodyguard tried to cover him, but it was to late. Both shots hit their mark. I drove away slowly and watched the panic. The guard didn't even know his boss was shot until after the fact. This sent fear into all the other lawyers, the news was having a field day with his death, and the two bosses were getting ready to leave the country after this.

The first one was the leader of the Devils Guards. He was gone before I had a chance to do anything, the second guy; the leader of the Nasty Ones was not so lucky. He was meeting with another lawyer in his Bar when I took him out as he was leaving to get in his car,poof..poof,the keys were still in the door when the cops arrived. The lawyer was a bag of nerves. The cops put him in protective custody because of fear for his life. Now the Bikers had problems to get help from any lawyers, and it was hard to get drugs inside the jails," But not impossible", with all the big shots gone, and the lawyers either dead or scared for their lives, the Biker war was almost at an end. They feared what and me I stood for, I still had another lawyer to get, and he was well protected with his own trio of body guards, but they were useless against me and my .22.This guard was wearing a bullet proof vest. He would start his car, open every door, checked all his clients for weapons, but you can't stop what you can't see.

One day when he was leaving the court house I popped him,poof..poof.. All the guards in the world could not save him. He died on the ground outside the courthouse. This act of boldness made other lawyers fear for their lives and sent the court system into chaos, the bikers could not get a defense lawyer at any price, neither could some of the other criminals. Majority of the court cases were postponed and the government was furious, but their hands were tied. They had no idea who was behind all the killing of the Bikers and their accomplices. Most of the lawyers that defended the Bikers were dead or in hiding. I was a thorn in the foot of all criminals, not only the Bikers, but everyone that had contact with them.

The drugs were quickly drying up and all the drug addict's were jonesing,robbing pharmacies out of desperation, and were caught on surveillance tapes with no problems. It seemed like everything was working out for me in my new job. No one was planting weed on the farms that I was watching, the cops were happy that there was less drugs on the streets and a lot less Biker activity such as intimidation of Bar owners and farmers, and a lot of other people that I knew nothing of yet. I was happy that I had to do less and less work, but it never really stopped everything. I cut it in half at the very least. The Police had made a connection and held a press conference to tell the public that they were making progress in the case of all the deaths of the bikers and their lawyers. Only I knew the truth, all they had was bodies and spent bullets. They had to say something to the press to make it look like that they were doing something. The general public was happy with the decrease in crime. When they were interviewed on the news, the only ones that were unhappy were the French papers who had nothing to print except nonsense, that made me happy, because that would glorify the Bikers and their activities by printing full color pages of dead Bikers,everytime the Bikers did something they would print it like they were hero's. The Bikers loved it at the beginning, but after I started my work the Bikers did not want to even hear their names in the papers out of fear that whoever was doing the killing would come after them next. The few Bikers that were left were working from outside the Country. After all it was an international drug ring. I was killing local guys but they were all over. They were afraid of who was out there. Then one day not long after the news conference, a French paper that was very well read, and did not like the Bikers, would constantly put pictures of the dead Bikers on the front page. They started to make jokes, like putting pictures of the missing Bikers on milk cartons with a text that read" missing if you see this guy don't call" a Ha! Not long after the paper came out, this reporter was shot by some want-to-be big shot, who shot this poor guy six times and he lived to I.D. the guy. He was probably caught and sent to prison with all the others. The prison system was so full they started to release all non-violent offenders and guys that were inside for fines and petty thefts with no association with the Bikers. Now it was at a point where the prisons were becoming Biker hangouts, a safe place to do business and get all the drugs they wanted. The guards were scared for their lives and their families. If they stopped the flow of drugs they knew that some of the guards were bringing some of the drugs in, but the bulk of the shit was brought in by guys they called "eggs". Now I decided to break a few eggs. The last thing I wanted was for the Bikers to have it easy, so I went back to work. I knew all the big suppliers and where they were. I just had to find the eggs. That did not take long; I had to watch the prisons on the weekends because that's when they would bring in the drugs. These guys called "eggs" would be threatened if they did not bring in what the Bikers wanted, so I was careful whom I picked. There were at least five guys bringing in drugs on the weekends. Two were forced to do so, the other three worked for the Bikers. It's the three that did this for money. I wanted, and I got my first egg as I watched one of the few dens that had what he was looking for like coke and Heroin, and Methadon.Then I followed him to his apt. Where he was getting ready to go back to prison. The next day that would be Friday, so I knew he would swallow the drugs before he left on Friday afternoon. Right after he left to go, I was waiting for him. Then as he got on the Metro and waiting for the train, I popped him in the head with a pool ball stuffed in a sock. He went right out, my goal was not to kill him just bring attention to his package. After I hit him I called the police from his cell and said I just took an overdose, I want to die. I gave his location then left. When the cops got there he was still out cold. When they ran his name in the computer they realized this was not just a regular guy with problems. After they checked him at theHospital, pumped his stomach and found his package he went to jail. He had swallowed over two ounces of smack and coke. Now instead of getting paid he's getting time. This act created lots of shit inside the prisons; with no drugs it wasn't fun anymore. Inside they were fighting amongst themselves and beating guards. I still had two more eggs to crack, after I found out who they were. I just waited until they were full, then I shot them not to kill, but to draw attention to their package. They were also arrested and put in jail. This time the cops were sure they had help, and held a press conference to tell the public.

The policeman that spoke gave the police this information. We now know that we are dealing with a vigilante. He or she has been involved in almost every death of Bikers or persons involved within the

Last seven months. We can only assume that the disappearance of some of these people that have not been found will never be found. We have made connections in almost every case. The only thing we can say with any certainty is that this person does not like organized crime. We will take this opportunity to ask whoever is doing this," it is a crime" and you should stop right away, because if we catch you your going to jail for a long time. One reporter asked what kind of gun was used? The cop answered we cannot give this information in fear of a copycat killer. If we tell you, everyone with a grudge will use the same gun to make it look like this person. The next day the newspapers were full, I hit the front page on every paper from Montreal to Vancouver to all over the states. The press just ate it up; soon they started running ads thanking me for my services. Another ad read, "Keep up the good work". The Government was fit to be tied. The police were very upset at me, but the public was in love with me and what I stood for and that made it contagious for me, and at that very moment I felt justified in what I was doing. I would continue my work as long as I had the support of the people. They could count on the Handyman to fix all the bad things that need fixing, including some things that are not right even though they are legal, like the Government's out look on Gambling, when the Bar owners had the poker machines, everyone made a few bucks. When they found out that the Bar owners were making money from these machines," they said lets make it illegal", then put their own machines, that's wrong, instead of a bar having one or two poker machines they have ten. Let me tell you, with all my surveillance of the bikers it was hard to watch as people that are on welfare try spending their last fifty bucks that they kept for food on a poker machine. I know it's an illness so does the government, and in my mind that's wrong, to take something illegal and then make it legal for them so they can take money from the poor. I started to watch some people that had a problem gambling and it was very hard to sit there and listen to these poor people telling strangers how their wives or husbands spent their whole cheque on the poker machines. Greed is a terrible thing.

I went to work, it's not something I wanted to do, but the problems were to deep to ignore as the government sat back and instead of helping these people by reducing the amount of machines they were adding more. These people were like Heroin addicts, it was very sad to see people in that state of mind where they have no control over their lives, and without a thought ruin the lives of the people they love so much. It's an illness or a cancer that will only get worse if it is not treated. So I started to give out counterfeit money by leaving it at the machines. Rolls of slugs, I know it's wrong, but by hitting the government in the pocket, that's where it hit the people. An eye for an eye! it's not helping the gamblers but it might draw the problem out of the closet and into the public eye. Meanwhile I had to go back to work. There was this one guy, he wasn't a biker but a native, he was selling whatever you wanted guns,crack,pot,booze,cigarettes.etc...etc...you name it, if he doesn't have it, you don't need it. This guy was in his fifty's and had no respect for the law at all. After I watched him for about a week it became very clear to me that this guy was a major importer of drugs and cheap booze. He had no fear of being caught by the police because he was native, and as he said "I don't recognize the white mans law", but he will when I'm finished with him. This guys a real jailbird. He must have been inside a lot when he was young because he was full of jailhouse tattoos, a lot of them were faded and just looked dirty, I'm sure it's guys like this that give natives a bad name. After watching him for three days taking a speed boat across the water full of boxes, on the fourth day he was crossing the river with another native and the boat was full of garbage bags. This was an everyday thing; he was always bringing something across. Then on this one day the cops started to chase him across the river in their speed boat the natives knew that all they had to do is hit the reserve and the cops would turn back, they had no authority on their land and the peace keepers would pretend to help, but everyone knew that they did not like the Police either, so the cops would lose almost every time until tonight as I sat there watching this unfold right in front of me I knew if I was not there the Cops work was for nothing, so I took aim with my .22,this was going to be a very hard shot, the boat was moving at a break neck speed, with the Cops right behind them but the longer I waited the closer they got to the Reserve. I was sitting; about the have way point on the bridge trying to get a good shot. It was almost impossible because the boats were almost on top of each other going from side to side almost to the point of ramming each other It was now or never. Then all of a sudden the natives fired a shot and the cops backed off a little, then I could hear the natives screaming like a war cry, just like they won the battle. I had to make this shot now. So I took aim without waiting for the perfect shot I fired at the driver bang, bang. just like always at least one shot hit the driver and the boat turned to the right very fast, then the native that everyone was chasing fell into the water, but the boat just kept going around in circles very fast, the Cops were trying to get the guy in the water but could not get close enough because of the other boat, it was clearly out of control. The driver was slumped over the seat, and the other native was in danger of being struck by a speeding, driverless boat. The Cops were at a loss. They had a man in the water but the boat could kill them or the guy in the water at any minute, so I took aim again this time I would aim for the motor bang, bang, bang, then ping! then kabang! The motor just exploded then fell off taking part of the boat with it, this was my chance to get out there, there was already tons of cops and R.C.M.P. and Peace Keepers all over both sides of the river, but they were to focused on the Boat and the other guy in the water to bother to look around for anything else. After it was all over the cops held a news conference the next day:" We have made a big drug bust on the River between the Reserve and the city, one native man is dead, another is in custody after a very dangerous and long chase on the water. They were importing five kilos of Coke and approximately six garbage bags full of pot, plus there was some illegal booze. The native who was shot was not shot by any police involved", then the reporter asked who shot him? Maybe his friend we don't know at this moment, we will know more after the investigation is completed. The Chief of the Reserve had his own take on things; this was not the way to arrest someone. I am sure that the Police shot this guy and was trying to deny it but there was no one else on the water but the police and the two guys that were involved. How do you explain that? After the autopsy was made it was clear to the chief and the police that they had help. They made a statement together, "it looks like the vigilante has expanded his work to include other crimes, this is for sure we have proof that it is the same person doing this; the reporter asked," how did the Vigilante manage to shoot this person with all the police involved in the pursuit?"

" We don't know that yet, we will know more after the investigation is completed." The Native that was arrested was charged with importing drugs for the purpose of trafficking and was given five years. The papers would not leave this alone, they were sure that it was a cop involved, how else could this happen? They would write: two guys in the middle of the river being chased by Police with no one else around is shot by the same vigilante that is shooting all the bikers, it looks funny, it raises a lot of questions. How did the vigilante know about these guys running drugs or where to find the Bikers or the Lawyers that he killed?" Smells like a Cop to me," the reporter said in the paper. I was the only one that knew the truth.

As time went on my life was almost normal, I had the money I buried so I was not concerned about my bills, but I was very careful not to over spend and draw attention to myself. I went out every day just like normal and always watching the drug pushers or the bikers or some other kind of criminals. My Wife was still unaware of my other job. As far as I was concerned she knew nothing. No one had any idea that it could be me. This made it very easy for me to continue my work. The bikers were still in operation, but were squeamish about showing themselves the way they use to out of fear that I could get them at any time that I wanted to. Most of the times they would get some poor guy on welfare that needed money to do their dirt, because they were so scared to do it themselves. I knew who was who, but they did not have any clues at all. They thought like the press, it must be a cop with a grudge. This was the same thing the cops were thinking; how else could all this happen with no suspects and no arrests. It had to be a cop with connections. They were so blind and only one minded, they were sure it had to be a cop. This was the best thing for me and the good cops because the bad cops were afraid to move, the good guys were watching everything and everyone that might have an interest in being a vigilante. All this extra attention was giving me a lot of stress. I was becoming grayer by the day; this is not what I had in mind when I was planning for my life. It seemed like every time I would think this would be the last one, there would be others. It was very stressful keeping such a big secret from my family.

Now the cops were paranoid, and everyone was a suspect. Plenty of times during my surveillance I almost got caught just by being so paranoid, everytime someone would look at me, or if the cops would pull me over for nothing just to do a spot check. It felt like my soul would leave my body and leave me just sitting there no matter where I happen to be. This was not a good feeling, it felt like everything else was normal and I was floating around watching myself from a distance. All I could do was talk myself back into my body. I could not seek help for obvious reasons, what would I tell my Doctor? I am the guy the bikers and the police want. I don't think so. I just had to deal with this new experience the only way that I knew how and talk myself out of it. Then one day I was watching the news just like any other day when the headlines said," A break through on the vigilante case" Have you seen this man? It was a rough drawing that did not look like me at all, but all the same I had one of those attacks. I could hear my wife way off in the distance saying Garrett what's wrong? Are you o.k? Garrett, Garrett answer me are you o.k.? Wow that was very scary. It was the first time that ever happened at home, after talking myself down, I just brushed it off and said," I'm sorry; I was in some very deep thought and could not answer you."

" You better get that checked out," she said I agreed. I found out later on the news that someone reported that he or she seen this guy delivering a package to the pusher that I blew up. I knew right off that this was a set-up; the package was left on the doorstep. It wasn't delivered so either the cops are grabbing at straws, but I doubt that, because if they put out a false drawing it would get them nowhere, so it had to be the bikers trying to draw me out into making a mistake, but I am not that stupid. I knew that any normal person would be curious who seen them and then return to the seen of the crime, so I did not want to disappoint anyone especially the bikers, after going through all that trouble of hiring someone to lie to the cops and give them a false I.D., of this guy. It would work in my favor; now the cops are looking for some fictitious guy that does not even look like me. The bikers just don't think first, so if they want to see me they will, but on my terms, because they still don't know that I already figured it out, but I wanted to let them know that I did.

I drove by the house that I destroyed with a very keen eye looking for someone watching the house. It did not take me long to spot what I was looking for. There was a guy sitting in a car about fifty feet from the corner, and I was right. It was the bikers, I recognized this guy from my surveillance on one of the bars that I was watching. He was just sitting there taking pictures of people that took an interest in the building.

It was time for me to make my move. I left my truck around the corner, took off my prosthesis then walked over to the site with my crutches and my fish knife. As I got closer I started to get that floating feeling again, but this time it was not as bad, but it was still there nonetheless. I did not need any more stress than what I was about to get. It was very nerve racking having to walk up to a car with a biker inside, and me with only one leg. I was counting on surprise. I was hoping that a guy with one leg would not make him feel threatened, and it worked. I walked right up to the car with my fish knife taped very close to my hand, then said to this guy in the car,"Parlez vous francais eh! Parlez vous francais eh!! The guy was so confused he didn't know what to say. I clearly caught him off guard. As I turned to put down his camera, I stuck him right through his ear with the fish knife. It went right in all the way to the handle; he just turned and gave me a last look then fell over the front seat. I quickly pushed him over and drove the car to the farm. On the way there his cell phone started to ring and wouldn't stop. It was getting on my last nerve, but I just let it ring and ring. After I got to the farm I buried him in a deep hole that I had made with the tractor along with his camera. I kept his cell and beeper. Then I drove his car two blocks from my truck and I left it there. After I got back to my truck the cell started to ring again, except this time I answered it."Yeah" the guy on the other end started asking," Where the hell are you? Your suppose to be watching the house!" Then I said, mumbling, like I had a mouth full of food," I went to get chow where are you"? Then he replied," looking for you."

"Give me five minutes." and then I hung up. But he was quick to call back after the five minutes were up. It was at that moment that I decided I was going to make contact. The cell was ringing and ringing then I answered, "Hello, who is this?" He said,

" It's me," I said he was very upset he said," who the fuck is and where is Jean?" I replied" Jean is gone to a better place." This made him even angrier, he hung up and then called back, I answered "Hello" and again he kept hanging up and calling back. Then his beeper went off. I was quick to return his call this time he said "Hello", and I said yeah it's me, this clearly made him pissed off, he said to me" What the fuck is going on"? Then I said consider this first contact and tell your boss to watch his ass, because I don't like shit and I plan to kill every one of you little pricks. Now you know my number and I know yours, then turned off the phone and the beeper, to give them time to think about everything that's happened over the last year and how many guys they lost to me. Then I took the cell and pushed *67 which returns the last caller, then the same guy answered"Hello"in a angry voice, I then replied! "It's me" after those two words I could hear the fear in his voice. The first thing I asked for was to talk to his boss, and he said that's impossible. I said if he does not call me at 6pm tomorrow I will kill one more of your guys, and if you don't think I will, just try me." I will talk to your boss tomorrow at 6 or else." This guy was scared and kept saying," my boss won't talk to anyone." I then hung up and turned off the cell. I went to the farm and made a little surprise for a biker named Bull Dog. He was very easy to get access to because no one knew that he was a biker but me. I took a log of firewood cut it on a band saw then placed a pipe bomb in side the log. Then put it back together and placed it in the woodpile. It was not long before he put that log on the fire.

Around ten o'clock the next night it happened, a blast

killed him and two of his friends. The wood stove acted like a bomb, turning itself into a very large grenade that sent shrapnel and hot coals throughout the house. At three the next day I called back, "it's me, where's your boss?"

" I don't know" he replied," I can't reach him."

" Same deal, if he does not call me by six o'clock I'll take a few more of your guys. Now I want the names of all the bad cops or I'll start all over and you can't stop me. And for your information, I already know who your boss is and if I don't get what I want the gang will pay." Then I hung up. At five fifteen the cell rang, I answered "it's me, hold on someone wants to talk to you." It was the boss.

" Yeah, state your business!" I said

" I want all the names of all the bad cops on your pay roll." then he replied "what's in it for me" I replied!

"You get to live". This pissed him off.

"You listen to me you little cock sucker we will find you and we will kill you, that's a promise." I just laughed.

Then I said," Just for being an asshole I'll kill two more of your boys. And if you don't give me what I want by 6pm tomorrow, I'll kill two more." Then I hung up.

The next morning on the news it was apparent that he took my threat for what it was worth, because the news was reporting that two off duty policemen were killed under suspicious circumstances, then later on that same day one more was shot and killed. It was determined later that all were biker related. By the time the dead line for the phone call came, they killed three bad cops already. Then at six o'clock the phone call came,"Yeah we can't help you the boss said, but we'll clean house ourselves" I replied

"Not good enough because I'm a cop and I know who's

who. You have forty-eight hours to give me what I want or I'll hit you again." Now they think I'm a cop, this will change everything. They started to set up all the dirty cops; I didn't have to lift a finger. I gave them forty-eight hours and in that time it was like watching a game of Dominos. The bikers were setting up all the cops they thought had something to do with the whole situation. The city was a real mess I did not realize how many cops were on their pay roll. Then the bikers leaked information to the press about this whole mess, they were saying it was a cop that was doing all the killing and they had proof. Of course the press fell for the whole ball of wax. The next day it was in all the papers, it read like this "Dirty cop is the vigilante" "Vigilante Cop is responsible for all the killing,"" Bikers confess that the killer is a Cop", so the bikers kept setting up the bad cops that they thought had something to do with all the shit. It was fun to sit back and watch them destroy a system that was most likely in place for years. The cops were very nervous, shoot first then ask questions. What a mess, they were killing each other like flies. Then I got a page on the biker's beeper, I returned the call, it was the boss of the bikers, he wanted to make a deal with me." How much do you want?" He asked,

" What makes think I want money? I have all that I need except for what I want, and that is a safe place for my kids to grow up, and as long as you continue to operate as a gang selling drug to minor's and corrupting the police, I'll be there until I feel it's safe." then I hung up. The next day the Mayor made a statement to the press. "I promise to do what ever I have to, to put an end to the biker violence, and to find this vigilante. I can not believe that all the those policemen were bad, but if that is the case then the whole city must be corrupt and I plan to call in the R.C.M.P. to conduct a investigation in the matters, and clean up this mess that as gripped the city over the last year. I also plan to get a anti-biker law passed so it would be illegal to be a part of a criminal gang."

Before that week ended there were more. The bikers gave the French papers a tape that had all the numbers of the Mayor's staff all at different times with the same hookers in the same hotel room doing drugs. This was a big scoop. The Prime Minister got involved, firing all the persons on the tape, then he made a bold statement, "If I find out that anymore officials are involved they will be brought to justice and prosecuted to the full extent of the law. If they are caught with bikers, they will be arrested like bikers." This made everyone very nervous. The bikers had no support in the upper ranks. The bad Cops were afraid the city councilors that were on the take was afraid that everyone had that fear of being associated with the bikers.

Now the Bikers were between a rock and a very hard place. Now they had to make new contacts with everyone fucking one another, they had no more trust for their own contacts after fucking all the bad cops and setting up all the city councilors. All their friends were running out, either dead or in jail, and the best part of this whole thing is that nobody knows who I am. Everyone thinks I'm a cop, which is a good thing for me because I must have struck a nerve. I did more damage since I started talking to these assholes then when I was killing them, they trusted no one anymore and it became very hard for them to do business, after all I didn't even make that last call, I just sat back and watched them destroy each other, the cops that they sat up sang like birds. The city councilors were both ratting on each other and anyone else that was involved.

It was fun to see their code of silence go right down the tubes. I can continue my work as the handyman and just do my job whenever I am called on with no questions asked. Now I have another problem, the bikers, or what's left of them, are turning to the mob for help, to import drugs and launder money, also there is safety in numbers with more than half their gang either dead or in jail they had no choice. All their connections were scared for their lives. At one point you could not get any drugs at all in my village, not even a joint, and the people who did get it most likely knew someone who grew it themselves. In my new line of work I always had my ear to the ground looking to keep the peace. Then one day down the road, after the drugs were almost impossible to find, I heard this young woman in her late 20's desperate to find some crack, she was willing to do anything just for a hit, it was very sad to see this woman with her whole life ahead of her so desperate to get stoned. Somehow I felt bad that she could not get her fix, after all it was me who dried up the supply. There was a rumor that she was trying to sell her little girl, a child of six years old. She was completely out of control and I knew that I had to do something, but what? My first move was to call Child's Welfare and I told them what was going on, but that was useless. They came and spoke to her and offered her a number for drug abuse and that was it. Then I heard one of the veterans that was always at the bar say "that poor girl was trying to sell herself to get drugs" and then she said,

" I have a little girl if you know someone, she's very cute." The very next day I heard there was a stranger asking about this young woman. He said he wanted to help her and wondered where she lived. I want to give her some money to help her. This sounded off an alarm in my head, you don't give a crack head money, call it a hunch but with all my new experiences something told me to watch her house. And it was a good thing this stranger was making regular visits to the girl's home and wasn't giving her money or food, but was giving her drugs. I knew this because she was trying to sell some crack to get cash. Who is this guy who would bring drugs to a crack head? I was sure he wasn't the good guy he made himself out to be. So I began to do some heavy surveillance on this woman's house because now she was a dealer and my first concern was not her but her little girl, so I kept watching the house every day and it just made me sick to see the condition of the little girl, she was very thin and had some bruises all over her legs. This was not the worst thing. The worst thing was the guy that was going to the house was a petty mobster that use to deal with the bikers, he was a real piece of work. His motive was not only to give her drugs.

After watching her house for a few more days this guy would bring older men to the house then the mother would leave then come back about one hour later. I had my suspicions about what was going on, but I had to be sure. So the next day I put a hidden camera inside the house, this was not very hard to do considering the circumstances and the experience that I had, I just waited for the right time. Two days later around the same time I watched the car pull up then Mob Boy got out and went to the house. Within five minutes he went back to the car, got some old man in his sixty's then went back into the house, then the mother left. At that point there was nothing on tape, then the old man started talking to Mob Boy, then the mobster left and waited in the car leaving the old man with the girl. This was my fear right from the beginning, but I had to be sure before I acted, but I had a problem, my camera was not in the right place, I could not see anything but deep down I knew what was going on but there was no proof. Within thirty minutes the old man left the house, got into the car and drove off. The mother was nowhere to be seen, so I went into the house to move the camera to a better location. As I entered the house I was very careful not to be seen because the little girl was still there alone. As I started to look around for the girl I started to get this bad feeling inside. I just wanted to get out of there real fast before the mother came back. I knew from watching the house I had less than ten minutes left before her return, so I had to work fast. As I entered the rooms one by one I came upon the girl, she was lying there on her bed naked, it was a disturbing sight. My first instinct was to grab her and run but if I did that the mother would call the police, and then they would tell the public. Then where would I hide her? No one knows me at this point; as much as it hurts me I had to leave her there. I set up the camera in the room. I'm sure the girl was drugged just by looking at little body in a fetus position on the bed. This sight would give me nightmares for the next two days. I had to do something fast, but what? I can't just take her but I was letting my emotions get in the way and that was dangerous for the girl and me. So I just waited for the mobster to come back, but this time I had the camera in the right place. I was taping everything, the mobster giving the little girl a shot in the bum, then when she passed out he carried her little body into the room and placed her on the bed, then he went out to the car and got yet another old man. By this time my emotions were unexplainable. I was so angry and upset that I could not just take the girl and bring her home that it was fogging my judgment. Before I knew it the old man was getting into the car, it was to late for me to do anything. This time I had proof. That night I went home and worked out on my heavy bag to relieve my anger. I worked out so hard that I thought I was having a stroke. After I stopped hitting the bag my brain was firing just as if I was being shocked. I could really feel the nerves firing inside my head. It was very scary and weird, but in a good way. After I stopped I got very calm and my mind was never so clear, that's what they must call a brainstorm because that's what it felt like a storm in my brain. Now with my mind so clear I had more of a plan. This guy Mob Boy was nothing more than a pimp of children. What bothered me the most was that I knew about the little girl, and how many more was there? This guy was selling kids, and I am going to put a stop to it. I had to follow him to see who was in charge so the next time he comes to the house with one of his freaks I'm going to take down some addresses, and get rid of the demand for kids. Then I'll take care of him and his boss. I was a little nervous because this was the Mob. But what's the Mob? I asked myself. Then I got the answer. It's a biker in a suit that's all, nothing more, nothing less. I found this guy by chance and if I am careful I'll do to them what I did to the bikers, cut them off at the knees.

First things first, this wasn't only a drug dealer but a real scumbag. So I went back to watch the girls house, but this time the girl was not home and Mob Boy went crazy. He had a old man in his car but no girl, he started to beat the mother and making threats, "she better be here tomorrow or else I will cut you off. There's a lot of crack heads in this world your not the only one" and then he slapped her so hard that she left her feet and fell to the floor out cold. After he got in the car I followed him and his friend to another place where I seen one of the other old men that came to the girls house coming out of his house, and he was upset also. Then there were two more guys standing by the door, Mob Boy was suppose to bring the little girl here, all his friends were upset that he did not deliver this girl. I could hear him telling these guys don't worry stay here and I will bring you a free-be and we will do this tomorrow I promise. The old man that was in the car with him got out and went inside with the others. I counted four guys, three older men and one guy in his 30's.This place must be some kind of meeting place for petit files, I just stayed there and watched from a distance. It was not long before Mob boy came back, but this time he had a young boy and girl both in their early teens. I got the impression they were prostitutes because they went into this place on their own after the Mobster dropped them off, then one by one the freaks started to leave in about an hour. This was clear to me now that the place I was watching was some kind of club where these guys could meet safely and have sex with kids, it was very upsetting to me to see this. After they all had there fun with the two kids Mob Boy showed up then the two kids came out and they were clearly drunk. I guess that's why Mob Boy was upset; he must have told these guys that he would bring the little girl. Now I know where all the freaks hang out and it's time to cut off the demand for kids. My thought is if these freaks don't ask him for the kids he won't bring them. The first thing I have to do is call my wife and tell her I have a big job to do and I'll be home in a couple of days, and she agreed just like always. This will give me the time that I need to do some surveillance and find out where these freaks live, and then I will deal with the supplier for these perverts. Meanwhile Mob Boy was going to get the little girl the next day, so I had to work fast so I left this den of freaks just for awhile to get the girl out of the house and away from the mother, so I spoke to a Nanny that I knew and made arrangements to take care of this girl. I told her that this was my sister's child and that she would have to let the girl live with her for about six months. I knew she'd agree. After we made arrangements for payments, I told her she would have to keep it to herself because the father of the girl was abusing her and the mother. She was more then happy to help. Now I had to get the girl and get rid of the mother. This was not hard. The girl was always alone at the house, but what do I do with the mother? If I just took the child the mother would call the police and I don't need that extra pressure of the cops looking for the girl just so they can give her back to the mother. So I left the mother a gift, it was a crack pipe laced with cyanide and a very large rock with a note saying "I will be here the same time tonight". It did not take long for her to take the pipe and crack, I watched from my cameras as she went through the whole process of making everything ready to take her hit. The first thing she did was put the girl in her room so she could get the best high with no interruptions from the girl. The minute she took the first hit she started to shake then fell to the floor she was dead in second. I rushed over to the house and quickly took my cameras and the girl who was so thin it was sickening, and the poor kid just hung on to me for dear life. It was a good feeling that I got her out of there. After I dropped her off at the Nanny's home I gave her very important information that said that she was not to tell anyone about this child and if they found out it would get back to the parents where she would most likely die of abuse, she agreed. I gave her five thousands dollars and told her there would be more if everything worked out, she was very happy. This old lady was on a very small pension so the money meant a lot to her and I knew the girl was safe. Now back to business and my job at hand. I saved the girl but there were many more kids involved that were being used for these sick fucks. So one by one I followed them, all together I counted eight persons involved with the club where the kids were being taken. This was the hardest job I ever had to do. Some of the things that I have seen are very sick and my mind will never let me forget those things, but it will give me strength to do whatever I have to do to deal with the memories that come with the job. The fact is I am developing just a little more respect for the good cops that have to deal with this kind of work that involves child abusers on a daily bases, it must be very hard for them and their families. I'll lesson the load for some of them if I can.

As I continue to watch the club it was becoming very clear that this was going to be very messy, because the more I seen, the sicker I became. I'm calling this place a club but it is more like a blind pig, not just anyone can walk in. It had cameras watching both doors plus a doorman who knew the regulars. Mob Boy was not a child molester but a dealer in children, he treated them just like he was selling drugs it was just a job for him, but not for long. In my first week I found out where all eight of these freaks lived and believe me they were from all walks of life. The more I watched the more surprised I got. They all had jobs and seemed like normal people.

When I started this I had visions of dirty old men hiding in closets, but that was not the case. Out of eight people was watching there were two very young men in their 30's,the rest were older men fifty and up. One of these freaks always came to the club in a limo and most of the time the last one to leave. This night I was watching Mob Boy getting shit from the guy in the limo for not bringing the little girl to him, I could hear the guy has he was leaving the club saying to Mob Boy "I already paid you, where is she?" he kept lying saying things like "she is with her father, it's not easy now". I knew it was bull because I hid the girl in a safe place but no one knew that but me. The Mobster promised him a replacement and told him tomorrow I'll get what you want. Now I had to follow the mobster to try to find out where he was going to get this other girl from, he must know other drug addicts that was like the girls mother that would sell their child for drugs, sure enough after following him the next day it was clear that most of the kids were from single moms that were hooked on crack or heroin can't help to think what would happen to the parents if they became sober. After Mob Boy got his next child for the guy in the limo they met at the club that night, Mob Boy brought a young girl, she might have been ten years old. The guy in the limo was very happy with her, I think he was just a broker, anyway, he took the girl and left. This was unforeseen, I wanted to catch him with his pants down, but instead he went to the airport, this made me angry that I did not interfere with his plans, and now this girl is gone.

It's time to stop this shit now before it happens again. In most of these cases where the child goes missing and the parents don't report it because they were sold for dope and guys like Mob Boy threaten to tell the police that it was the parent that made the offer if anything was said. So the parent is afraid to say anything out of fear. I wanted to go to the police with the tape that I had but I felt that after dealing with the bikers I had no trust in the police. I am not saying that all the cops are bad, but the question was, which ones are good?

My first order of business is to get rid of the pedophiles that I know of. I already know where they all live through my surveillance. The first guy was a 35yr old school teacher who teaches special education classes for the slow learners. After he left to go to work this day I entered his apartment with the plan of killing him when he got home, but instead I found a hidden room behind his book case, the stuff I found in that room was sickening. There were snuff tapes of kids, a lot of them. One of which I recognized. It was a young boy that went missing about a year earlier and the parents were pleading on the news for his safe return.

This stood out in my mind along with a few others, not all parents were drug addicts. This boy's parents never gave up hope. I felt that I had a duty to tell them about their son so they could move on and get a peace of mind, but how? The boy's father was very depressed and the mother turned to the bottle and was drinking very heavy, mostly because of the police suspecting them, they had one-track minds. They had no other leads and had to blame someone. The whole family was destroyed because of this prick and his per-versions. I wanted to tell the father because I would like the same courtesy and closure. So I made my first phone call to the boys Father." Hello, Mr. Jones you don't know me but I think I can help you, just listen carefully."

" Who is this?" he said? Then I replied!

"You must let me finish before you interrupt me again, I have the man who took your son and if you want him you can not tell the police about this phone call or you may never find out the truth, I already have the man and the proof that you will need." Then he replied

"Is this some kind of sick joke or do you want money?" That is when I told him the truth. Mr. Jones listen very carefully, I am the man the press calls the Handyman vigilante I am calling you so that you will have closure. Your son is dead and I am sorry about that, but you can have the guy that did it. I'll call you back in 24hrs. This will give you time to grieve and to think of what you want to do to this freak, I will give you all the proof that you will need, but there is one condition you can never see my face and if you agree to this I will pick you up at a fixed location and bring you to this guy, if you tell the police anything I will know. This is between me and you and the freak that killed your son. He asked {sobbing) "are you sure it's my son and how do you know that he's dead".

" The only thing I can tell you is I am sure, other wise I would never have made contact with you. I will call you back tomorrow at the same time. Mr. Jones I can't tell you enough that you must keep this a secret or you will never know if I am telling you the truth. The only way to know is to trust me, and I know this must be hard to take all at once but we must work fast or he will kill again. I will call you at the same time tomorrow and one more thing don't tell your wife I know she drinks very heavily and she could jeopardize this for you and me, after we are finished I will take care of everything then you can tell your wife, but not before. I will talk to you tomorrow." Then I hung up.

The next day I went to work, somehow talking to Mr. Jones gave me a sense of justice, like I did the right thing even though I knew it was wrong. I felt this man deserved to know after, all he has been through. I waited for the freak to leave work. Then I waited for him in his apt, in that dirty little room. After he got home it was just a matter of time before he opened the door to his room. He had rap music playing very loud that just made my job easier". I hate rap" when he opened the door he had a surprise. The room was very dark except for a light from the other room shinning through, but the only thing he saw was a hammer. I smashed him right in the teeth, it sounded like glass being smashed through a bag. He hit the floor like a bag of wet sand. I quickly tied him up in his chair, and then told him what I was going to do. He was crying and begging for his life, the blood was pouring from his mouth. His teeth were all busted and jagged. Then I took the tape of Mr. Jones son and put it on and made him watch it and then told him it was time to meet his Father. I called Mr. Jones and said" it's me, have you thought about what we talked about?" he answered in a very somber voice," yes sir I have, but why are you doing this?" You will know more when we meet. This is what I want you to do; there is a small village just north of where you are. You will take a taxi to the corner of Grand and 19 ave,then you will go behind the Bar in the parking lot. There will be a small green car there with tinted windows, you will get inside then you will put on a hood that I left in the front seat. After that you just wait and I will show up. If you are not following any of my instructions to the letter, I will know, and I will call it off. Just sit there and wait. I was already in the car, but he did not know that. After he showed up he came and got into the car. As soon as he put on the hood I spoke to him. Don't panic Mr. Jones it's me you must stay very quiet and all your questions will be answered at the right time. This poor man was terrified. He did not know if I was some kind of weirdo or worse if I was going to kill him. After all I just told him his son was dead, and I was this vigilante and I had his son's killer." I would be afraid myself", but I kept talking to him as we were driving to the freaks house. I was telling him that he did not have to kill this pervert, that's my job. But I want you to do whatever gives you satisfaction from this. When you are finished with him you will say to me that you are finished. Then you will put the hood on and I will bring you home and we will never speak of this again do you understand? He replied with his voice shaking" yes sir I understand". Then as I pulled up I told that we were here. He got very nervous and started to shake uncontrollably and kept saying "I am sorry sir. I'm sorry. Then I gave him the last of my instructions. After we are inside it will be very dark and I will be right behind you at all times. You'll then watch the tape and when you seen enough you will tell me. Then you will meet this freak, do you understand? He said with his voice shaking," yes sir". I sat him down in a chair in front of a T.V. Then I put on the tape and told him to take off the hood. The tape was barely started and he began to sob," That's enough, turn it off, please turn it off". I told him to put on the hood and remember what I said," yes sir he replied", when I am finished I will say so, then I will put on the hood". O.K. I said". Then I put him in the room with the freak and closed the door. I heard Mr. Jones crying and the freak screaming. So I put on his rap music that he loved so much.Mr.Jones was in that room for over an hour. Then I could hear him say" I am done" in a firm voice. When I opened the door my first thought was what a mess, the freak was dead. He must have suffered a lot; I don't think I have to tell you the details if you are a parent. You can relate or put yourself in the same room with the freak that killed your kid. What would you do to him? Whatever you can think of Mr. Jones did it. And one thing for sure he won't abuse no more kids. I then took Mr. Jones by the arm and led him out to the car, where I went on to ask him if he was o.k. He said yes sir, thank-you sir for your help. Then I asked for his keys to his home, then I told him that he must never speak of this to anyone after I drop you off, do you understand? He said" yes sir". I'm going to drop you off at your house, but you can not take off the hood until I'm gone, and don't forget I know you, but you don't know me so you must keep your word to me, or I'll be forced to deal with you for my own safety. I did this for you so you would have peace of mind, I hope you get that Mr.Jones, now get on with your life. Then I went back to the house to get rid of the body. After I got there I could see what I have done. It made me sick to see that kind of mess. I felt very bad that I told the Father about this freak. Now the Father will have to live with that on his mind for the rest of life and maybe beyond that! I'll never do that again, from now on it's business as usual. I'll never involve anyone else, I will handle it myself. The only way to clean such a mess is by fire; after all I don't want the Cops finding any fingerprints that could link Mr. Jones to the crime. Now I had to get the rest of the freaks that I knew of. There were at least seven more from the club plus Mob Boy, and if I don't move fast enough it could be life or death for someone else's child. These guys have an addiction to children," It had to be that", no normal person would do such things.

After doing this last job it left me void of any feelings of guilt towards my victims. It left a mark on my soul that was never there before. I wanted to get these guys more than anything else. I never felt so much hatred towards anyone but these guys. My next job was the old man that I seen abusing the little girl. I went to his home and waited for him outside. When he showed up he was with Mob Boy and another little girl. If I act now I could jeopardize everything, but if I don't I could endanger the girl. I knew when Mob Boy brought children to this old man there was a time frame of about an hour. The minute Mob Boy left I sprung into action. I ran as fast as my legs would take me to his front door, and I started to bang very hard like there was something wrong. The old man came to the door still in his coat." Yes can I help you he said", then I replied," yes do you have a little girl here? The look on his face was pure fear. He turned and started to run for his phone. I then started to scream like a maniac as I chased him down his long hallway. He reacted by screaming to "please don't hurt me, please all the time grabbing for the phone and trying to dial it, I grabbed the phone out of his hand and struck him with it in the head, as hard as I could but, he was still screaming and trying to kick me. The blood was running like crazy from his head. Then I kicked him with everything I had, right in the knee. It popped like a firecracker; the pain was too much for him. He just passed out gas as he lay there on his marble floor with his head bleeding and his knee completely broken. I started to look for the girl, when I found her she was half nude in the bathroom, like she was waiting for him. I had to hurry; I only had another 30 minutes maybe less. I went back to the old man and choked him to death, now I had to get him and the girl out of there before Mob Boy got back. It's not easy to move dead weight. I dragged him to the back door, and then I went up to the bathroom to get the girl. As soon as I opened the door the girl grabbed on to me like she knew me for along time, her arms tight around my neck. I ran with her down the stairs and into my truck. Now I had to get the old man into

The truck, this was a lot harder than I expected. I dropped him twice and on the third time my heart was pounding so hard, that I could hear it in my head. Time was quickly running out for me. I had less than ten minutes left to get out of this without being seen by Mob Boy. Finely I put his body in the truck and drove away. As I was leaving I could see Mob Boy's car coming down the street, he passed me. I was never so relieved not for me but for the girl I had in the truck. This is a very stressful job, now I'm stuck with another girl, I had to call my nanny friend where the other girl is, and find out if it's o.k. To bring another kid, after all this was a spur of the moment thing. I did not expect to do my job with a kid in the house. I knew that the woman would be happy to take care of one more child. After I confirmed this, I dropped off the girl who was sleeping at the time, {most likely from drugs}. I told the Nanny that her parents were abusing her and I took her to protect her life. I told her that's why the girl was sleeping because her mother was giving her pills to keep her quiet, and I had to get her out of there. If the police found out they would just give her back to the parents, that's why this has to be between you, and me, she was more than happy to help. I was more than happy to give her as much money as she wanted. I then told her that I would come back with more cash for the extra child. She said; "you don't have to do that, you already given me enough, if I need more I'll let you know the next time I see you".

Now I had to get rid of that body, I took him to the farm and just like some of my other victims, put his body in the wood chipper, then buried his remains in the compost. After cleaning myself up I went home and seen my wife just to tell her that I love her and spend a few hours with her before I went back to work. After leaving her some money I told her I would see her in a few days. She told me she loved me and missed me and I shouldn't be working so hard. I felt bad about lying to her but what else could I do? It was a white lie, meaning I was lying for the better. I was not cheating or doing drugs; I was killing killers for the betterment of lives of others. I had a lot more work ahead of me and the faster I did it the less chance there was for someone else being hurt or abused. My first concern was where did Mob Boy get the little girl? Were they drugged up parents or an innocent family? I would have to watch the news for that answer because to much time as passed for me to follow this guy, now I would just have to wait and see if it's like the other girl, there will be nothing on the news, but if she was kidnapped it would be all over the news. So I went back and waited at the club where I found Mob Boy standing outside talking to another man that was sitting in a car, but this was not a freak, I had the impression that this guy was giving the orders, because Mob Boy was clearly upset and was telling the guy in the car that the old man fucked off with the girl and what should he do. Then I heard the guy in the car say don't worry just tell the mother that the old man took her to Disney World and they would be back in a few days until I figure out where the old prick went, if she gives you a hard time tell her you will cut her off. Now I have my answer already it was drugs again, this time I had Mob Boy's boss, I followed him to a garment factory. I will keep this in mind while I am taking care of business. I have to deal with the other Pedophiles first. Already knew where they lived but I was surprised to find out that they were from all walks of life. Maybe that's why the Police never caught them. But I had the supplier and his boss, plus eight pedophiles that were involved with them, well now there's six left.

My next job was a hockey coach. He was tamed compared to the other two, but a freak nonetheless. This guy was very hard to get close to. I watched his apartment for two days but my hands were tied because there was always a steady stream of young boys coming and going from his apartment, at will he would take them to restaurants then go back to his apartment. After Hockey practice they would go to his place, not all of them, but the same few all the time. I can't help to think where are all the parents for these boys? They all can't be druggies. I just had to wait and wait and wait. I was getting tired of watching the boys go in and out all hours of the day and night. After two days of watching this guy it was time to make my move. That night about five boys were coming and going, when the last boy left I went to his door and knocked softly, he thought it was the last boy coming back, because he unlatched the door in a hurry and said, "come in, what did you forget?" before he even had a chance to turn around to see who was at the door, was on like a dirty shirt, I quickly put a nylon rope around his neck and was choking him, it seemed like forever. As I watched his face go from white to pink to red, to a blue, then his eyes started to bulge right out of his head, after it was over I hung him from the ceiling light fixture with the rope to make it look like he killed himself. There was no reason for me to remove the body; I just left the front door open a little. I knew the boys would find him the next day and call the Police. That's when the boys would confess to being abused. How else could they explain being there?

My next job was number five, this freak worked as a volunteer at a hospital. It was hard to say how old he was, I am guessing forty years old, I'll know more in a day or two.

I decided not to go back to the club, not only for safety reasons but I had all the information I needed on the pedophiles. I knew where all of them lived and Mob Boy was the Pimp that would bring them their fix right to the house. On the second day of my surveillance I seen Mob Boy's car pull up, this time he had a young girl around twelve years old with him, after talking to her outside the car for a few minutes, I heard him say to the girl, "I am going to go for a hot dog I will be back in an hour, and I'll be parked right over there" pointing to a spot near the park, about 300 feet away. This girl must have been here before because she went running right to the apartment on her own like she knew the place. I didn't know what to do at first, I did not want to hide another child, but I had to put a stop to this sickness.

I made a decision it was time to let the police know I was involved, if I don't, these Pedophiles will just continue to buy sex off of pimps like Mob Boy. It won't be Mob Boy I will take tonight along with the other guy; God knows what they would do to this young girl. I took my .22 and just waited for Mob Boy to come back, I didn't have to wait long, when he pulled into the parking spot I threw a rock at his car to get his attention, the first one missed then I threw another I was just trying to get him to open his window. I did not want to break anything, I missed again, the third rock hit his hub-cap, PING, it worked, at first he got out and looked around, then he got back into the car. Then he put his window down and started to look up and down the street, when he started to roll up his window I fired, poof, poof, poof, no noise no mess he just fell over in the front seat. Now I had to get the other guy, I was just waiting for the girl to leave. I only left myself a window of five minutes because as soon as the girl got back to the car the shit would hit the fan. I had to work very fast; the minute I saw the girl starting to leave I went into action as soon as she was out the door.

I was at the door with my .22 in hand, then I knocked, when the door opened, I was in shock, it was not a man but a woman it threw my concentration right out the window. I hesitated just for a second, then she started to run for the phone, I took aim and fired.poof, poof, both shots hit her in the back of the head. Then I left, running all the way to my truck, as soon as I got to my truck I could hear the young girl screaming, then I seen her running back to the apartment where the Pedophiles were. I got out of there before she found the man. The next day it was all over the news and in the papers. The police had the girl in custody, but she was in shock and could not tell them anything, but they knew it was my handy work by the. 22 and then they told the news that it was the work of the Handyman. There were all kinds of questions: Why was the Vigilante killing these people? The Police said they would hold a press conference tomorrow after they have more information and a chance to talk to the girl. Meanwhile the papers were printing all kinds of things like: "Handyman strikes again", another paper wrote, "Watch out the Handyman is coming". The Police were very angry and at the press conference they said over the last two weeks we have five bodies that is the work of the Vigilante four of these people had previous criminal records for Pedophilia and sexual misconduct. The fifth person was linked to organized crime and also had a record for sexual misconduct. From what we have seen this person has no fear of the bikers or any other criminal gang. He is now killing Pedophiles from the pattern he has shown. We are asking this person to stop at once. This is the highest murder rate that the city has had on record. While the cops were calling it murder the press was calling it justice. The French papers loved me, the front page of the paper the next day they printed, NEXT in big bold letters and went on to say how crime has taken a nose dive since this person has been taken out the trash," first the bikers and then the Pedophiles and the last one had links to the mob. I say good for him and keep up the good work. I support you along with a lot of the public. Since this person has been active in taking out the scum of the society it's a much better place to live unless you're a bad guy.ha, ha!" He wrote. Now with Mob Boy dead and six of his customers dead, Mob Boy's boss must be shitting himself along with the other Pedophiles from the club and I have to get them before they move on out of fear of being next in line. The boss who was working out of the garment factory was no boss of anything just that he was laundering money for the Mob that was his involvement along with being a pervert broker.

My next job involved a member of that club still he was no ordinary member, he was also a member of the city council, and it would be wrong if I just shot him, the people of the city might think that I was out of control. So I just sent him letters at his office telling him what I knew. At first I didn't hear anything at all then all of a sudden he quit office. This caused a lot of speculation with the press who did not know anything about his activities with the kids. They were saying things like "he was involved with inside trading and giving favors to family members to get building contracts" and things like that. After a day or two he killed himself. He left a note saying that he was abusing children and the only way for him to stop was to take his own life. In the note he said he was sorry for the pain that he has caused. That did it, now the press was going crazy with speculation, how could such things happen in Government office like the Mayor's Council? The Police made an investigation and found the letters that I wrote, someone leaked a copy of the letters to the press, each one was signed The Handyman. Now the people were sure I was a Cop, how else would they get copies of the letters to put into evidence? This was working out better than I expected, the papers were writing how I killed this man in power, with a pen not a gun or rope just words. Now I had to get back to business at hand, there were still two Pedophiles left from the club that I had been watching, both were men in their late fifty's. The first one I wanted to get, I wanted to give him a very public and very messy death, hoping that it would send fear through the rest of the Pedophiles just like I did to the bikers. Fear was my best friend, it seemed when someone got scared they would go into hiding and were afraid to come out, and that seemed to work very well for me in the past. I was like the invisible man; no one knew who I was or who was next. That's fear, not knowing anything. Not even the cops knew anything; there were no clues at all just my .22 and my name The Handyman. I decided that I would stay my course and keep it as clean as I could. The man I was watching worked out of his home and every now and then I would see different kids going there, but they always left after a short time, what was this guy doing? The kids that went there did not look like the rest and he was a very nice guy, he did work in the community with the kids like giving them things that they needed, such as clothes and food to help them out. Maybe I was wrong about him, but I never killed anyone for nothing.

After watching him some more it did not look like he was abusing any children from what I could see, and I watched him just like the rest. Maybe I scared him straight, I hope so. Now I'll go to the next freak, and come back to him because I have my doubts. But I'll be back. There was one left, plus the guy in the garment factory and this guy worked for the mob. So I'll save the best for last.

I went to the home of this last freak and did my surveillance just like always. I stayed there watching for a day or two, but this guy, a man in his fifty's was not alone he had help and it was very clear that there was something going on in that house. His helper was a young man about eighteen or nineteen years old that would go out and bring back young boys and girls all of them were no more than and from what I could make out they were all either run aways or already turning tricks. The ones that were turning tricks were always coming and going. I noticed that there were two kids that came home with the younger man; I am guessing they were run aways because he picked them up at a bus terminal. I was watching the house for two days after he brought them home and they never left. This concerned me, even though there were one or two regulars that came and left on their own. Then the boy that lived with the old man left and came back with another youngster. I am not sure if it was a boy or girl, I could not tell by the way they were dressed, but like the other two, never left. It was time for me to get a closer look. The house was a triplex and the blinds were always shut and the basement had windows covered in blankets. So I could not see inside, and now with the third kid going in and not coming out, this was a very big concern to me, and I made a decision to enter the house. It should not be to hard to get inside and because they drank a lot it was a safe bet that they would not hear me if I was careful. So that night around midnight when I knew they were asleep I entered the house through the basement window so I would have the element of surprise. As soon as I got the window opened the smell was over whelming, I could hardly breathe and it was so dark, could not see anything. My first thought was I entered a cesspool of some sort, I started to flick my lighter just to get an idea where I was stepping, so I wouldn't fall into a shit hole, as I kept flickering my lighter to look for some kind of light, then I seen one of those hanging light bulbs with a string switch. I pulled it and a very dull light came on, it was not much brighter than my lighter, but better than nothing. At first I could see nothing but shadows of coats hanging up in one of the corners of the basement. I kept looking around for a cesspool so I would not fall in. The smell was overpowering to the point of where it was stuck in my mouth, just like I was in a cesspool. This was very un-nerving. I just wanted to get out of there, it was that bad. I had to keep looking around, and with not much light it was very hard to see anything at all, but I pushed on and kept looking. Then as I was backing into another room constantly looking at the stairway and listening for any noise at all, I bumped into what I thought was a coat hanging up and when I turned to push it aside, I got the shock of my life, it scared me so bad that I jumped back and fell into a pool of jellied blood, it was the body of one of the kids hanging upside down, his head was cut off and his genitals were missing. This sent me into the worse panic attack I ever had. The more I tried to get up the more I kept falling and slipping in the blood that was like jelly and was stuck all over me. My heart was pounding so hard that I thought that the people upstairs would hear it. I needed air fast or I was going to pass out, but I could not just leave. Then to make things worse I could hear someone walking around upstairs, this just made my attack even worse. I rushed over as fast as I could and turned off the light and headed for a corner to hide. With no light it made me panic even more my heart was pounding like crazy, I was sweating like a mad man as I felt my way around flicking my lighter to get enough light to get my bearings. I tripped over another body and fell into a pool of blood and guts, this boy was gutted, and all of insides were all over the floor and now all over me. It was just to much for me to take, I yelled," oh shit!" not even concerned about being heard anymore. The old man heard something because he was coming down the stairs with a stick or something in his hand, I could see his shadow getting closer to me with the light shinning from upstairs down behind him. He was saying, "Who's there? Is anyone there?" so I made a grunting and moaning sound like a wounded animal. Then all at once the basement lit up like a ball park then I was blind for a split second by the bright lights, I could see him coming down the stairs, so I made another noise," uhhhhh," this was working he came closer to me, he had no idea that anyone was in the basement. Just as he got within about ten feet from the coats that I was hiding behind, I jumped out and grabbed him but I fell with him, he didn't know what was happening, he was trying to scream, but I kept grabbing him around the mouth the whole time we were sliding all over the place. I was covered in blood from head to toe. The sight of me that way must have scared him to death, he must have thought that one of the kids came back from the dead, because the more he tried to scream he could not. The only noise that came from him was an ohhhhhh sound. After I got my footing I punched him with a right fist across the his face so hard that he left the ground and came down on top of one of the bodies that had been gutted. He lied there mouning, then I pick up his stick then cracked him right in the head his head. It opened like a melon, his brains and everything else that was in there was now on the floor. His blood was oozing from his ears and every other hole that he had in his head. As I sat there recovering from the struggle and listening for the boy that was up stairs, I was looking around the basement in disbelief. It was sickening, it looked like a slaughterhouse, and the bodies did not even look human. What kind of mind was I dealing with? It was not only the old man; I still had to deal with the nineteen-year-old boy that was still asleep. I slowly crept up the stairs making sure I did not wake the boy. It was unbelievable, the house looked so normal upstairs it was a wake-up call. I never would have guessed that this carnage was going on here.

As I headed for the boy's room I passed myself in a mirror. It was the scariest thing to see myself in that state. No wonder the old man couldn't scream. Then I came to the boy's room, he was lying there asleep and beside his bed was a half case of beer. I had so much anger from seeing what I seen I did not know what I was going to do until it happened. I sat on the edge of his bed and quietly woke him up by shaking him on his arm. As he turned and looked at me he went into a fit, the fright just consumed him, he could not scream or yell or even fight he was swinging his arms, but they were like wet noodles, he had no strength at all. The sight of me in the state that I was in was enough. Full of blood and guts from head to toe it must have been too much for him to bare, he just passed out. I picked him up like a fireman then threw him down the stairs, he was not dead, but I was sure I broke something when I tossed him; he was still out cold when I got to the bottom of the stairs. I kicked him a few times in the face for good measure, and then I went out to the truck and got my .22 and shot the both of them, two shots each in the head.

Now I had to get out of there in a hurry the smell of the dead was firmly planted in my lungs and my mouth at this point. I did not know if I would ever eat again.

The worse thing was still to come. I had to get home from here. It was now 3 a.m. If I get caught driving home in these circumstances it's game over. I had to get to the farm and fast. I wanted to look for the girl, but I felt it would be a waste of time after what I seen, so I took a wet towel and removed what I could around my face and took off my clothes, put everything in the truck and left.

On the way to the Farm I could not stop thinking of the horror that I just seen, and I seen a lot. I put guys in wood chippers and killed lots of men, but this was different, it was sick. What kind of person could dismember kids and have them hanging in a basement? What was he going to do with them? The things that I seen tonight will stick with me for the rest of my life. I had to call the police. I got cleaned up then went to a phone booth and gave the cops an address and I said to the cop on the phone

"This is the Vigilante. You better bring a lot of body bags. I just killed two freaks, but they killed plenty of kids. Their bodies are all over the basement." Then I hung up. That's the first time I had contact with the cops. It went from my mouth to the cops and right to the press. Outrage was the only word that made any sense. The police were outraged and disgusted at what they found at this house. The press was told that this was the worse case of murder and Pedophilia they have ever seen. They found the remains of three boys in the basement, and in a freezer there were more remains of at least five other kids that have been cut into pieces. And there could be more. Plus they found the owner of the house and his son both shot dead from the Vigilante or the one they call The Handyman.

The Press could not let things go for at least six days, there were police and news reporters at the house and almost every day they found more remains. Some were buried and some were hanging in the garage being cured with salt. The Mayor of this town ordered the house to be torn down after the police were finished. I let myself calm down for a week or two before I went for the guy in the garment factory, he too had something to do with the Pedafiles. I remember him talking to Mob Boy at the club when he was bringing the kids there, but like Mob Boy I think he was a broker or a better word is a pimp.

After a two-week rest the media was still speculating on who I was. They were asking the police how they knew it was the Handyman that killed those two men in the house. What was the connection between them and his other victims? A detective answered this time;" He called us and told us where to find the bodies.

"How do you know it's the same guy?" a reporter asked.

"He left his trade mark to let us know that it was him, and so far there was no connection to the bikers as far as we knew, but what we do know is that this guy has killed a lot of people in the last sixty days. He has killed at least seven Pedophiles that we know of, and we know that it is him because of his trade mark." A reporter asked,

" How is it that this guy can find all these criminals and kill them, but the police can not even arrest one?"

"If it was not for this guy how many more children do you think would have died?"

"We can not be everywhere. Yes this guy might have saved future abuse, but he is committing murder in the process. We hope that he will call us and report the crime instead of taking the law in his own hands; after all we are the law. We can deal with any crime without killing the suspect. That's all I have to say for now, thank you, there will be no more questions." Now I had to get the big guy in the Garment Factory, so I did just that like I have. I watched him for a week steady, not only at his work but also at his home too. I wanted to find out everything that I could about this guy. The first thing that I noticed was that everyday at the same time there would be someone bringing Garbage bags to his office. At first I thought it was clothing samples, because there were a lot of bags every day. There would be a different guy bringing one or two big green garbage bags. I knew that he had ties to the Mob, the question was how deep. I had to find out what was in the bags. He never left with them but he was always making deposits at least twice a day. So I put two and two together, he was laundering money for the Mob that was his job, besides being a child broker. The more search I did on this guy the more connected he was. It's time for me to spend some of that money that I buried on some surveillance devices and a few second hand cars. Now it was time to make the Mob pay big this time. I found that there are worse things out there than petty crooks and Bikers. Anyone that would sell a child to a freak is one of the worse kinds of criminal. They sold them just like meat, and the worse thing was it was for money, nothing else just money. I have seen a lot of shit since I have become The Handyman and let me tell you something, some people would do anything for money, and I do mean anything. The Bikers and the entire killing that they did, and all the lives they ruined, it was for money. The Mobsters were selling children to Pedophile who would do god knows what to them. All for money, that's what everything, is about money, the more money you have the more friends you have, that's a fact. All the fighting between the gangs was not over power or drugs it was over money. Just like the Mob, they were selling kids just like meat. It was sickening to see but it was all over money. So it's time to pay the piper. The money that I took I spent it on spy gadgets, that I might use, like enforced goggles, telephone lens for my camera, night vision video, and some listening devices. It might come in handy. I went back to my wife and spent a few days home and gave her a thousand dollars. I told her that I had a very big job to do and I would be back in a few days. Of course she agreed it was work and my bills were being paid. Just like always there's nothing different in my life as far as she is concerned. I work I get paid, just like anyone else. I'd stay a day or two and did some more work around the house. Down at the farm where I had to clean out the barns, and take out the old shit and hay and put fresh stuff

Inside. This was a good smell and I was glad to smell it, and I would never complain about the smell of shit again. After what I just went through with the Pedophiles. Now I had to get back to business at hand. There was still this guy at the Garment Factory; I knew that he was laundering money for the Mob and that he was a child broker. We call him a Pimp,because that's what he was. I'm sure that he was doing his share of abuse. The more that I watched him the more I learned. All the garbage bags that were being brought to his office were not garments at all. It was money, lots and lots of money. That's why he had to make deposits every day, twice a day on some days. This guy was a family man. He was married and had two kids in their teens, a boy and a girl. He was fifty something, but the Mob had him by the balls. You either did what they said or they would do something to your family. Now the question was, how deep was he involved? Was he a willing participant or just scared to say no to these guys. I had to find out how deep he was involved and try to get some of his bosses, along with him and the guys bringing the money to him. I watched the Factory for a week just to get an idea if they kept the same time frame every day; it was just like watching a time clock. Every day at the same time one guy would show up with a garbage bag, go inside ten minutes later, he would leave, within two hours. The guy from the Factory would get in his car with two brief cases. He'd make a deposit at one bank, then go to another and do the same. This was an every day thing, I could set my watch by him and his Mob friends. After getting a few rolls of film on these guys, I got the system down to where I could tell you who was coming that day and at what time. My next move would be very ambitious on my part. There was so much money involved. What I seen could solve all the health care problems, and most probably build a new Hospital in every town if you had to. There was that much money involved. The only way to get the attention of these mobsters is to hit them in the pocket, because that's where it hurt most. The way I look at it this way it was put in my lap by some higher force. It seemed like just from simple surveillance from following Pedophiles, I fell on this warehouse where this guy who was some kind of child broker or middle man turns out to be the guy who launders all there money through this very large..(Garment Factory).

Now listen carefully, one night as I sat in my truck after everyone left. I waited for the security guard. He was a man about seventy, that I said hello to every night since I started to watch this place. He was very accommodating to me, always polite and liked to talk. I entered the building to head right for these Pedophiles office to have a look around. Maybe plant a listening device in the room, but I got the shock of my life. It's not what you think, there were no bodies, and no blood, in fact there wasn't anything. There were garbage bags, as many as you could put in a fifty-foot long room and twenty feet wide, without falling on them. It was very full, I bent over to throw one of these bags aside and it ripped. To my surprise every bag was full of money. Each bag weighed approx:fifty pounds,now I had a very big problem. How many could I carry? I had my prayers answered this night. I had my truck and I loaded it with about fifty bags of this money. Then I went to the Farm and looked at what I got. As I opened each bag I was thinking Oh God. By this time my plan of killing the Pedophiles that I was watching made me scared to think of what I fell over. The first thing that I did was burying everything but ten bags that I made a promise to myself. When this madness first started, any money made from my new job would only be used for good, and believe me that's dirty money that I just took. I removed about fifty bags and that did not even make a dent in the room. It would be awhile before they noticed. I am sure this was one of the safest places to keep money. Who would rob a Garment Factory? Right! Meanwhile I was sitting on ten garbage bags full of money, and nothing smaller than fifty's and nothing larger than one thousand dollar bills. All of the money was old and used; it was not made yesterday, which means it could trace. I made ten letters of all the same content saying," this money is a gift from the Handyman if you tell the Police they will take it. If you spend it freely, it will be taken from you, either by the crooks or the Police who the money belongs to. There was no loss of life at the time I took this money. Use it wisely towards helping the poor; there will be more. If you're careless there will be less, signed, The Handyman. The first thing as to be clear is, that money fell into my hands. It was the last thing I expected to find. I'll give it all to a very good cause. Then I will go back to work before they find it missing. I started with the very small poor Churches; there were ten in all. All from the same area, very poor, and they needed all the help they could get. This made me feel good even though they would have to spend it carefully. The people who suffer the most will benefit, most of the money has came full circle. Now I had to get back to work and get one of the mules that was bringing the money to this guy, or they will move the operation. This Factory must have being doing this for a long time, if I could just walk in and walk out with fifty bags of money in the dead of night. The thing is if they put guards and all kinds of security. The Police or a simple crook would want to go in and find out what they were protecting with all that security. With out it, no one asked any questions, so this must have been in operation for years. Now I blew it, if they find the money gone before I want them to, it will screw up the whole thing, so I had to work fast. If I take out my first mule they will attribute him to the missing money. His name is Louis and every Monday at 5:45 he would bring garbage bags to the Factory, to give it to the guy that was washing the money. This guy was a Jewish man that had some taste for young boys, that's how I found him and his Factory. My first order of business was to get rid of Louis, so I watched him about 20ft from where he was parked. Every time that he came I pretended to be sweeping the parking lot next to his spot. In my hand I had my Blowgun and a dart that was eight inches long and very light. As soon as I seen him coming I was ready. I got next to another car and took aim, I had to get him before he got out of the car, or it would attract trouble. The very second that his door opened he did not even have time to turn and get out of the car. The door opened and I fired, there was no noise at all just the dart hitting the side of his head. He quickly fell over to one side. I jumped into action. I pushed him over and drove off to the farm with his body lying there in the front seat. Blood was dripping out of his ear from the other side of his head, the dart went right through.

I drove approx: 70km to the farm, about half way the dripping was driving me crazy, drip, drip, drip on the floor of the car. Even the radio could not stop the dripping. I was so happy to get to the farm and get out of that car. You have no idea, it is the little things that bug me. After I took him out and buried him. I drove his car to the airport and left it there. Hoping that after awhile they would think that he left with the money. Things got very bad when Louis did not show up at the Factory when he was suppose to. The Mob went into panic mode. They called the guy in the Factory and asked what happened to Louis? The Jewish man that I was watching from the beginning was in deep shit. The phone calls kept coming every five to ten minutes," did he get there yet". The Jew would answer" no I haven't heard anything yet'. The guy on the other end of the phone must have been the big boss. Then the Jew made a call back to the boss who was very upset to say the least. He said to the Jew," I hope your calling me with good news" The Jew said no Mr. Franco just the opposite, we are missing money. What the fuck are you saying to me; talk English, What's going on? That's when the shit hit the fan. The Jew went on to tell the boss Mr. Franco, that they were robbed, what do you mean robbed? Someone took a number of bags from the Factory, How many Franco asked? It's hard to be sure, I'm guessing at 30 bags, plus one that Louis never brought.

The Mother fucker Franco said, where were you all this time? If I find out you had anything to do with this, you, and your fucking Jews, who did you tell about the Factory? No one, the Jew answered. There's no reason to start calling names. Check Louis if you find him, you'll find the money, that I am sure said the Jew. For now I am safe, they think the mule took the money, but I better watch Mr. Franco. He is the key to all the money, which means he is the Mob boss. I focused more on my surveillance on him, now that I knew he was in charge. The only way to see him is for the Jewish guy to make it happen. All my surveillance is in and around the Factory; I have to get some kind of bug on him to find out where he lives. Meanwhile the mules kept coming and the Jew kept making deposits, but now the Jewish guy was shitting himself. I'm sure that since Louis disappeared and the money was taken, it was time to line his pockets. If he did not do it before, he'll do it now before they move the money and kill him. That is almost a sure thing, once they lose trust, that's it; they even killed the old man that was guarding the place. The Jew was next, I was sure. I started to pay more attention to the boss and what he was up to, after following this guys car after he left the Factory. I got a lot of information from a listening device that I put in the car of this boss. This guy was not what I expected; the Mob boss that I was expecting was an old man. He was always giving orders, and the guy that I found was a young man in his thirty's. He was well dressed and had a very dirty mouth. The more I found out about this guy, the more I learned to hate him. During one of his talks with another Mobster I heard him say" If the Jew tries to leave I want you to feed him and his family to my Dogs." I don't trust this fucking Jew. Starting Monday we will move the money to another Factory." Which one the other guy asked," the sock in the east end. Now I wanted to tell the Jewish guy, but he got himself into this shit. It was his family that concerned me. He has kids that most likely are Dog food if I don't get involved. So after finding out where the boss lived, I put more bugs on the phone conversations. This got me more info then I needed but very helpful. It tears me apart knowing that I have all this info, and can't give it to the Cops and let them do the work. If I did that there would be no work done at all, and the Mob will always be strong because of their ties with the law. I heard this guy telling this guy that they had to meet at the regular place and should bring his friends. The time was 8 p.m. Well I was ready to go but where? They did not say where the meeting was taking place. So I had to follow the old fashion way. It was safe as long as I did not get close. Things like this made me nervous, when I did not know what I was getting into. Like how many guys were coming? Where was I going to end up? This drove me crazy. All the listening devices in the world were now useless. Unless I find out where the regular place was. So I followed the boss picking up more info as I followed him around. Then around 7 p.m. the boss started to make calls. There were ten all together. Some of the calls were to other Mobsters that I reconized.Others were to Cops, I knew this because when the boss made the calls he was always very angry, yelling about everything. This time he was yelling at the guy on the other end of the phone.

"He said listen to me the meeting is at the regular place 8 o'clock, that's one hour from now, be there". The guy said I can't, I'm on duty. That's when I knew it was a Cop. The boss insisted you just fucking be there or I will kill you, you piece of shit.I don't want excuses. After he finished calling the ten guys I had to follow him. He was already a wreck from not knowing who fucked him for that money, and there were only a handful of people that knew where it was. Now he was going to find out. One of the people that were going to the meeting was the Jewish man from the Factory, but my guess is that the boss had all the ten guys that were going to the meeting followed. Hoping that one of the guys would run, and then he would know who stole the money. After following this guy all over, we ended up at an arena where there was a kids Hockey game going on, as I sat there and watched the boss he was watching to see who showed up as they went inside one by one. I couldn't tell how many of his guys were there by sitting in the car, and it seemed like he was in no hurry to go inside, so I went in ahead of him and sat by myself and just waited. At 8 o'clock on the nose he walked in and went right to the section where the others were waiting. As he started up the stairs to head where his friends were waiting for him. I was not to far away, but far enough not to draw attention to myself. There were a lot of people there for the game. Mostly the parents and friends of the kids that were playing, there was a lot none the less. The boss and his ten guys were in a section where nobody sat, at the very top of the arena. I was sitting one section over. The place was very loud with the screams of the parents yelling at their kids. No one was paying any mind to the ten guys being yelled at by the boss. He was yelling at each guy and then all of a sudden he slapped one guy right in the head. The guy stood up very fast as if he was going to strike back. The boss was so mad that he was going to shoot him right there, but the others interfered. The boss went on screaming like a mad man, but no one at the arena even noticed the yelling. After the yelling stopped everyone shook hands and started to leave. So I got up and went as fast as I could go to my car. I wanted to find out where the boss lived. This was my chance. I sat in my car and waited for him to come out. The others were leaving. I knew most of them from watching, but there was two there that I seen but didn't recognize. One of them was the guy that got slapped. After everyone left there was still those two guys left and the boss. My impression was that they were waiting for him, but he was the boss of the Mob. I'm sure he did not care about them or anyone at this point. He was being robbed and crossed and had no idea who was doing it. These two guys were looking for trouble. I could feel the tension in the air. They just sat there in their car just like me. Then the boss and his bodyguard came out of the arena. As the boss stood next to the door the guard went for the car. As he got half way across the parking lot, the two other guys that were waiting for him started to leave their parking space. Driving towards the door where the boss was waiting, as soon as the guard noticed the car he yelled to his boss. Then the two guys stopped the car got out and started to fire. Killing one of them right off, the other tried to jump back into the car and get away. The boss was on him like glue. It all happened so fast that it was surreal, like it was slow motion. The boss seemed to walk very fast up to the get-away car and started to fire. The windows were breaking and the blood was everywhere. He got in the car with his bodyguards and started to drive off. They slammed on the breaks, the boss got out and started to fire at this car in the lot, all the windows broke. I was confused, whom was he shooting at? I had no time to get out and look, but I'm sure it was a wittness. Now I had to follow him but that would be impossible with all the shooting that went on. He would be sure to be watching that he was not followed. So I went in a different direction just to be safe. I had this feeling that the

Jewish guy was in danger but there is a old saying" when your involved in organized crime blood in blood out. Which means in for an inch in for a yard. There was nothing I could do for him and from all the surveillance that I done his family had no knowledge of his involvement with the Mob. As far as they were concerned he owned a Garment Factory. If it were not for his involvement with the Mob, he would be an outstanding member of Society. But I knew better now, I had to get the money and take out another mule before it got too hot. It was clear that the Mob boss was not afraid to get his hands dirty after what I seen at the arena.

The next day I took another mule, this time I killed him and left him for the Police to find along with the money. This would give me the time I needed to focus on the boss. This really hurt the Mob after I shot the mule with my.22 and left the money. Now they know that I am involved and the Police will start to look around even more. They will watch the Factory very close after finding a body in the parking lot with a car full of money and proof that the Handyman was involved. This made the boss mad, to say the least. He got a hold of a bunch of guys that did work for the Mob and told them they had to move the money fast. So the next night a moving truck backed up to the Bay doors and started to load the money in the truck, but the money was hidden in boxes of Garment's. I called the Cops and told them someone was stealing from the Factory. I knew they were just waiting for me to call after leaving my trademark on the mule. In minutes the Cops had the place surrounded, but the guys on the truck and the Mob boss had no idea that it was the Handyman that killed the mule. The Cops found the money in the Garments just started something very big the Mob was fit to be tied. The Cops were showing off all the money they found, and were looking for the Jewish man that owned the Factory. He was hiding the minute I shot the mule. He left with his family on a plane the same night. If he didn't the boss would have shot him for sure. The Cops held a press conference saying" The Vigilante has struck again this time. He has given us this very impressive load of cash. That will take weeks to count and even longer to find out who it belongs to. None of the persons arrested would talk to the Police. Only saying that they were hired by phone and were to get an address after the job was completed by phone. They knew of nothing that was in the boxes. Now let me tell you something I just struck a blow to the Mob that would have all kinds of repercussion down the line. The boss was freaking out, he was shooting people that were working for him for nothing. Just out of paranoia, and to think that it was the Handyman that did this. It made bad things worse. Who is this fucking Janitor? He asked one of his guys. One of the Mobsters answered: it is the same guy that fucked the Bikers, no one knows who he is, and it's not the Janitor. It's the Handyman. This pissed off the boss, what are we going to do? The Jew fucked off. We have no access to the accounts. Now let me think we need cash we have some in reserve, but that means we have to liquidate some assets. We have the suppliers to pay to get our shit. This fuck is dead! I want you to find him and kill him this fucking Janitor. The other Mobster said it's not the Janitor, it's the Handyman. Well the boss went off, he started to beat this other guy then he shot him once. Then he said "Handyman is that right" and then he emptied his gun into this guy. Now he's killing his own guys out of fear and anger. This was a big mistake on his part, after that he could not even get a bodyguard for himself. No one trusted him.

The next thing that he did surprised me. He got in his car and went to a Restaurant and shot two Cops that were sitting at the booth eating. Then he went to the Jewish man's house and set fire to it and went home. His lived in a duplex on a small road just north of the city, where there was three other houses, all belonging to other members of the Mob. Now he had to regroup and he had to give answers to whoever was in charge. He was the boss for here, but he had to answer to the big boss who was not happy at all. With the turn of events, they lost so much money. The big boss who lived somewhere in Columbia was coming to meet him. I heard him tell this guy that lived on the road with him, that there was going to be a big meeting. Now this other guy that lived on the road did not know that he was involved until now. Which leads me to believe that all three houses are Mob owned. The guy I am talking about lived there with his family and was a welder. He had a nice big shop where he worked all the time. He never took outside jobs; every time I called him at work he would say," have too much work and I'm not taking anymore". After checking around I found out that this guy was a weaponeer in the United States Navy. Now I am getting somewhere, this was the guy that made all the guns and bombs for these guys. He kept a very low profile and no one knew but me. I hope so, so one night while I was waiting for the Mobster to make his connection with his boss in Columbia. I went looking around his shop after he left. What I seen was incredible they had old torpedoes that were hung and they were not used for sinking ships, but importing drugs. They had their own motors a GPS system the whole bit. That's all they had to do was program in the coordinates and put this thing in the water. It would go anywhere they told it to, after it got to where it was going. A ship that was already in our waters would just pick it up and empty it and send it back for it's next load. Each Torpedo held a lot, maybe one or two tons of whatever they needed the possibilities were endless. They were very smart at some things. They would surprise me by doing something stupid, like keeping bags of cash in unsecured locations without security. That's the price you pay. I know now how they bring their drugs, what to do with this information? I think now that maybe the cops might take the information. The question is, how do I explain this whole thing to the cops without gettingcaught? Everytime I make contact they have one more piece of me either on tape through the 911 calls or maybe just good police work. I try to be careful but sometimes in the heat of the moment your just not there. So I think the press would be my best bet. The other question is, how at this point I am more popular than Elvis was? The press just loved me, every time they did a piece on me they sold double. It didn't matter which paper printed The Handyman, it meant big bucks to them. French, English even the International papers made money on my name. It was like phenomenon for this whole year. I broke the backs of the bikers killing most probably a lot. I don't track, but I am sure that it is at least one hundred. Got rid of at least 10 Pedophiles and a whole bunch of bad cops. There's still more that I find out about everyday as I watch and deal with the Mafia, and to find out the Mafia are not even in charge. It's the people with the money that are in charge and that's not Italian or Greek any more. It's young guys all thirty something and from all backgrounds, and they're there for the bucks. So is everyone else, that's why it's so hard to decide whom to give the information to. This is a major find. I think I'll just go on being me by myself, if I get someone else involved it could be my down fall. I will continue the way that I have, and like my father use to say," IF IT ISN'T BROKE, DON'T FIX IT." I know if I go to the press the cops will raid their offices looking for evidence. I don't need that, and if I call the cops who know where the information will end up. Meanwhile I am still watching and listening. The boss of the Mob had no clue that I had bugs in the car and on the outside of the windows. While I was listening one night after the event at the arena, he was pissed as his bodyguard. He was telling him that he should not go around slapping guys like bitches in front of other guys.

There will be more hot tempers." We were very lucky last night that it went in our favor. It could have dangerously gone the other way."

" We have to be calm, the boss answered"

" We were calm. We kick ass, they tried to pop us and we turned the tables, tough luck on their part.

"Where is that fucking dick with my information?" Then the phone rang.

"Yeah" the boss answered.

" I got Louis's, car they found it at the bus stop empty." Well this pissed him right off. He started to talk about killing the Jew's family, they had nothing to do with anything but he wanted to send a message.

" No one rips me off. First Louis and then the Jew. He has family here. Kill them first, get Louis's brother, he works in an office, I have the address." Then he went on to give the address to his Hench men. It's a good thing that I was listening. I quickly got into my truck and went to this guy's office; he was just a normal guy that worked eight hours a day, forty hours a week. What he did not know was that there was some killers coming for him. They're going to kill him just because he's related to Louis, but not if I can help it. I know where he parked his car, where he worked, and where he ate, I just had to watch him.

Now I'm going to do something about the information that I have about the welder, to send my own message to this prick, but first things first. This guy's life was in danger and it was partly my fault for killing his brother. As I watched him for a day it did not take long for his Hench men to make an attempt on the brothers life. As I sat there watching the brother's car while he was working, two guys pulled up in a white van. One guy got out and slid under the car, he was planting a bomb. What they did not know was I was watching from a distance in my truck with my .22. As the guy under the car was fucking around putting the bomb, I was taking aim. I shot him twice as he lay there under the car. His partner was getting edgy when he did not come out. The van was parked right in front of the car and the driver heard nothing and could not figure out what was taking the other guy so long. Then he got out and walked around the van to see what was taking so long. I could hear him say "hurry-up your taking to long", of course the other guy didn't answer he was already dead, but his partner did not know that until he got on his knees to see why his partner was not responding, then I took my other shots poof, poof, then I drove away. It would only be later that the cops would find these two guys, one dead holding a bomb under a car and the other dead beside the same car. Now the cops will protect the brother. I have to draw attention to the welder because that's a big blow for me, and a bigger blow for the cops, now that I hit the two guys that were trying to kill Louis's brother.

The Press, who's always waiting for a story involving the

Handyman, grabbed this one like hot cakes." The Handyman kills two more Mobsters who attempted to kill someone else with a car bomb," then they had pictures of one of the Mobsters slouched over his dead partners feet that were sticking out from under the car they were going to blow up. The police are holding the owner of the car in protective custody. This made the mob boss very mad now that he knew that I was involved. It made my work a little harder. I just kept listening to my bugs and the more that I listened the more information I received.

His next plan was to kill some of the Jewish guys' family. These were people that had no connections to the mob or the Jews. Only to be related by blood. So I went to this very large home in the rich end of town where the Jewish man's brother lived, he was a doctor and had a family, a wife and two boys in their teens. This guy had no clue what was about to happen, and neither did I. I went there to see who the boss was talking about killing. It ended up in a firefight with three guys from the mob. It started by accident. I heard the car coming up the driveway I had no weapons on me at all. I was just going to look at the time. I had to act fast or there would be some dead people that didn't deserve to die. I have to think, there are three of them and they came to kill. I am there just to look, but things changed in a blink of an eye as they drove up the driveway very slow. I ran up behind them, crouched down as low as I could get so they wouldn't see me running up behind them. I still didn't know what I was going to do. The car stopped and one of guys got out and ran just ahead of the car the he ducked into the bushes. The moment the back of the car came close where he ran into I did the same. I ran right behind the guy into the bushes. I was directly behind him as he turned to see who was there, I punched him right in the chest then his gun went off, POW! It was a 9 mm, the noise was deafening, and he fell to the ground. After dropping the gun rolling around in pain and unable to talk I took his gun and popped him. By this time his friends were coming back, and all the lights went on in the house, they were stunned as the car peeled backwards towards me. They thought I was their guy they swung open the door and were yelling "get in" I opened fire POW, POW hitting the driver. The other guy started to run down the driveway towards the street looking behind him trying to see who was shooting at him. As he was shooting back towards me I was lying down on the grass beside the driveway. I fired two more shots pow, pow, the first one hit him good, he lifted right off the ground, the second shot hit him in the chest.

I had to get out of there. I could hear the cops coming in a hurry. My best bet was run up the street and wait for the bus. I got the gun that I used so I don't leave any prints; if I get caught I am fucked. I waited for the bus to come. The cops came first. They pulled up right in front of me at the stop; they jumped out and were yelling at me to get out of there. I just ran as fast as I could. I never looked back. I was never so relieved. After I stopped running I took the gun and wiped it clean and threw in the sewer. After everything calmed down I went back to my car to get home, it's been a rough two days. I am just getting started. This Mobster is not afraid of me, he's just mad because no one knows who I am. No one would ever suspect me of all people, please, as long as I don't say anything and don't leave any witnesses, it's all bad guys getting fucked one after the other and the press stays my friend I am safe, so now I have to get the welder if the cops find that, their going to brag big time. After I grabbed a few days rest I enjoyed my time there. Then it was time to go back to work, now I had to take my .22 and leave a clear message for the cops and the mob. I am the Handyman and I am everywhere. I stuck up on my friend as he was welding one of the very large Torpedoes that he had just emptied. This was the same case as the factory. Everything is low key. I just happened to find him on my way through the heap. I fired two shots, poof, poof just as I fired he started weldering, so I fired again poof, poof, then all at once and singing, the blood pouring out of his eyes and out of his mouth and he was just singing b.i.n.g.o at the top of his lungs then he gurgled for a few seconds, then he realized he was shot. He started running towards me I fired poof, poof, both hitting him in the face; he did not want to die today. This was a very hard kill, I shot him four times before he started singing and twice after, all headshots, and he was still grouning, this scared me a lot. I will bet you that the Mob boss will be shitting bricks.

This is so big I have never seen so much dope in my life. The very next day the cops and the press were all over this very big story that I gave them, and it went like this. The police held a press conference to announce the biggest drug bust ever made. Just in the metal shop they found three tons of Heroin and the means of importation, which was fascinating to the police. The welder was identified as a gunsmith that worked for the U.S Navy and was released on misconduct, (Unbecoming for an officer).

The others that I killed were also identified as part of the Mob. Then they announced "this very large bust that we have made as given to us by the Vigilante they call The Handyman. Well that did it, the press had a field day every paper had front-page coverage of the bust with photos of the dead welder slumped over his handy work and just behind him stacks of heroin, but what the police did not know was that the boss was living three houses away. I wanted to deal with him myself after all the smoke cleared and everything was quiet. I called my little friend the Mob boss and said "Hi it's me" I could feel the fear over the phone as he paused before he answered:"yeah, what the fuck do want from me"

" Your life of course, what else would I want." Then he said "I can give you anything you want, just name it. If it's money just say how much". I just laughed and said,

" Nothing gives me more satisfaction then to see scum beg, but that can't help you because I want you dead so I can feed you to your dogs like you have done to others. I will do you. Good-bye." Well he was shitting now. I tied up all their money, I cut off their drugs and at least half of his force was dead. I had the public's support and I was starting to win some of the cops over, which believed in what I was doing even though it was wrong. I have given them more criminals in the last year then they could ever hope of finding. The difference is I don't have to follow the rules or the red tape so that gives me more freedom to do my job without interference from the law or paid Judges who most likely would turn down request after being paid off by gangsters, and it happens all the time. That's why the criminals are always ahead of the law. I still had a lot of work to do. The mob boss, even though he was the boss, had to answer to others above him because he was just too young to be running everything. My guess, after watching these guys for so long, had to be a family affair. I never heard him answer to anyone, which will be a lot harder now that I got the Welder. I made contact with him by making a threat, now I fear that I'll never know who the real boss is. I guess I will just have to watch and wait and see what comes up to the surface. After making the call to the boss and getting him upset this would be the best time to keep track of all his movements and phone calls. I need to know who is the real boss; I am sure that he or she is not in the country, but patients is a vertue. Sure enough within two days of the big event when the police put the grab on the welders shop and confiscated all the heroin, now they were watching all the ports and waters around the country now that they knew how they were bringing in the drugs. The police that found the welder contacted the U.S. government and told them what to look for so now it will be a lot harder to move the drugs but not impossible.

After listening to a few more conversations of the boss and his contacts I heard him say it has to be done by air. Even though that's all I heard I knew it was not over, I only got the later part of the phone call. I would have to increase my surveillance by double which would not be easy considering the sircumstances.With everyone on the alert and afraid to speak on the phone, it was very hard to figure out what his next move was, but I had a lot of time and equipment to help me with my task and my next job. After watching and listening for days I finely found out how they were arranging for the drugs to come in. The boss gave himself away when I seen one of his guys going to his bar that he owned, then passing him a letter as soon as he got that letter he had to leave. This was important for him to move so fast, but I still had bugs everywhere including his car and that's where it happened. I heard him talking to the guy who brought the letter. He was telling him where the drop was going to be. They were going to drop a bale of smack on the farm and he should go to the farm and warn Jimmy and that they couldn't call each other anymore because of all the shit that's happened, so from now on all contacts will be by mail or in person, no more phones until they can find a better way to deal with their problems. Right after he said that the guy that brought the letter left the boss went back to the bar. So I followed the guy to a restaurant where he went inside. I quickly jumped out and put a locator bug on his car because if I followed behind him he would see me for sure, he was warned to be careful. And that he was but I had a bug with a ten-mile radius planted, now I just had to follow the beep. I had to make sure I got there before he left other wise I could be following this guy forever. The bug that I planted was just a locator beacon and I had the receiver in my truck. It was not something that was right on. The louder it got meant I was getting closer, but I still had to rely on my eyes. It started out o.k. As I followed the beep for about an hour and a half, that the beeps started to get closer together and got louder I knew I was getting close, then all at once the beep stopped so I just kept driving around the area looking for that car that had the bug.

After I checked two or three farms on the next farm just as I was driving by the driveway I could see the car leaving. I took note of the driveway and kept driving to the next town about twenty miles away. After it started to get dark I went back and parked the car a good distance away and started to walk. As I came closer to the farm it was clear that they did not want any visits from anyone. The whole perimeter of the farm was fenced in with barbwire and the farmhouse was run down, but all the fields were plowed and kept very well, it looked like a regular farm but I knew the truth. Whoever was living there took care of the farm so it would look like it was a working farm. They had cows and pigs and were growing hay and wheat and some corn. This farm looked no different from the others but I knew better. I did not know what they were up to but it had to be important to be all the way out here. The more I watched the more suspicious it became to the locals. I had to find a better way to watch this farm without being seen, so I left and went home knowing where the farm was. I started to form a plan. There were three farms next to the one that I had to watch but I could not approach any of the farmers out of fear that they could be with the guy that I want to watch so I decided to go back and get a closer look but this time I took a remote control airplane that I bought with the biker money and put a camera inside. After I made my first pass with the plane everything looked normal, all I seen were crops everywhere. My next pass I got closer to the house, now I was getting somewhere. There were trails leading from behind the house to a large barn that had smaller trails coming from the other three farms. This meant that my hunch was right. All three farms were connected by these trails and all the trails lead to the barn that was hidden in the bush behind the farm. Now, what were these guys up to? They had three farms one right next to each other. If I did not follow this guy I never would of had any suspicions about these farms, it all looked normal. They had no dope growing, the only thing that was out of the ordinary was that the farms were runned by the mob or bikers or both, and that barn had something inside, but there was no way for me to find out what because of the connecting trails. There were to many questions and not enough answers. What was in the letter that this guy brought to the farm? It had to be big for them to go out to this place because it was very remote, and there were no witnesses to anything that I could make out but I had to be patient. I kept a close eye on the farms for almost a week. Then on my last day I was going to stay.

The Postman drove up this long driveway and started to beep his horn. Then about an hour later the farm came to life. The trails were buzzing with 4x4's going back and forth from the houses to the barn and back to the houses, this went on for about two hours. Then everything stopped all at once except for one 4x4 that was pulling scrap wood and a trailer full of Hay. My first thought was that they were going to light a fire for a air drop, but after watching for awhile it was clear this was a form of communication but to who? After they lit the fire and it got very high they put the hay on top and it had to be wet because the smoke was very dense and with no wind it went straight up, this was a signal for sure. Not long after, about thirty minutes two small airplanes flew over the farm and they were so low that I took the numbers from one of the planes, the other was far inland behind the farm in the woods, but at tree top level, I guess it was to avoid radar, but nothing happened that I could see, then after it got dark I went on the farm starting from the road, I walked in towards the bush with nothing but my fish knife and a broken kite just in case I got caught I could say I was getting back my kite. But the kite was a weapon, also the small cross pieces of the kite were sharpened to a fine point, and the kite itself was very strong cellophane. I also had about five hundred feet of one hundred test fishing line. As I made my way on to the farm I headed for the barn that was hidden in the bush. I really didn't know what to expect after I got there, but whatever was going on it was in there, those planes had to of

dropped something even though I did not see anything. But what did they drop, Money or drugs? As I got within view of this very large barn I could hear the roar of the 4x4's coming up the trails. It sounds like about five of them. I just laid close to the ground as quiet as a mouse as they passed me and headed for the barn, they were all riding with no lights, they knew the trails good. After they all passed me and entered the barn, I got up from my hiding place and started to wine my fishing line across the trails. One line every sixty feet and there was one on every trail just in case I had trouble leaving. After setting some of my traps I went to look at the barn, this was no barn. As I started to get a look inside, there was nothing. No bikes, no people. It was empty, what the fuck is going on? I seen them come in here, where did they go? Just as I was saying that, it happened. There was a small crunch, then the floor inside the barn started to lift like an elevator. Then I heard the roar of the bikes. They were coming from under the barn. I quickly tried to find a place to hide close to where I was so that I could see what was going on, so I hid just near the door where I could see inside. This was unbelievable. Every bike had a trailer packed tight with camouflage tarp. As all the bikes came out of the ground they pulled into a spot that had a large door on either side. I counted seven bikes and nine guys. I couldn't make out what they were saying, but then the owner of the farm that I was watching seen something on the wall where I was standing. As they talked I had seen one of the guys run towards the door where I was. Must have tripped an alarm, the next thing I knew I was running through the bush with a very large pit-bull running after me. The whole place came to life. All the bikes were unhitching the guy was yelling, "Hurry-up". The dog got his scent then everything slowed down just like slow motion. I could feel the dog on my heels snarling like he wanted to eat me. I could hear voices all over the woods they were coming for me, and I had to get out of there no matter what. So the first thing I did was I stopped running and turned to my left as quick as I could to head for a trail and find my way out. Just as I did the dog grabbed my leg and was locked on, but he did not realize that he had my prosthesis quickly took a piece of my kite and stuck him right in the ear. He died very quick. I still had seven very mad gangsters coming for me all I could think about was not getting caught, but the faster I ran the closer they got. Then one of the guys must have hit one of the lines, because I heard the bike go flying through the bush and crash. I could not see what was happening behind me except for a few flashes of light and the sound of shots going off and bikes revving. I was too scared to look back, but the only way out was in so I stopped because I had the advantage. There were no more dogs just a bunch of guys on bikes. I had to think fast, they were all sticking to the trails because of the bikes. I have some trails booby-trapped. The rest was up to me. I stuck close to the trails, and then came two bikes one behind the other. They passed me at a very fast speed, the first bike hit my line and the guy's head came right off and the bike kept going like nothing happened. Then the second bike saw the line and turned very hard to the right and the bike flipped over. As the bike was flipping I jumped up and chased it. After it stopped, the guy that was riding it got up and was confused, his left arm was hanging off at the elbow. I quickly put a stick from my kite right in his eye; he kept trying to grab me with his bloody stump. I then gave the stick a whack and he fell over. I jumped on the bike and took off with no lights.

I had to get to my truck before I felt safe. I was buzzing along at about 45mph in the dark of the woods when all of a sudden one of the others were waving a flash light to get me to slow down thinking I was one of them. I slowed to the point of stopping. As he came to me he kept saying, "did you see him",

"Yes he is right there," I said pointing behind me. As he started to go in that direction I knifed him all over starting at his neck and head. He had no chance to yell for help. Just then I heard aloud crash then another. The bikes were hitting the lines and then leaving the road, I had to go check and finish what I started. If the bikes were off the road that means they are on foot and most likely hurt or headless.

With three guys down and the crashes I just heard it would be five, but I must make sure that they are all dead or tied up or they could call for reinforcement. And that would be the last thing I needed at this minute. My heart was pounding almost out of my chest with all the gangsters chasing me. I am still unsure how many are left, but I have to go back and finish what I started no matter what the consequences are. As I started back up the hill sticking to the woods I could hear at least three guys talking in very low voices. I could not make out what they were saying, but I could hear them getting closer, there foot steps were getting faster and their voices getting louder. I could hear small twigs snapping under their feet as they approached. My first thought was lay still and let them pass but my choices were limited. It was kill or be killed. It's a good thing I have the advantage to see them and they don't see me. Just like an animal I looked for the weakest one first. He was a big tub of shit with a big mouth, and a 12-gauge pump. The others still able to ride, the big guy was on foot and was no more scared then I was. I could smell the fear from him. As his friends left to go and look for me, little did he know that he was next. As he started down the trail I followed him very carefully until I saw my chance. I knew it would not take long, as soon as he sat down I would kill him. Just as he leaned back on a tree and lit a smoke he continued to draw on that cigarette, I got that much closer, when I got about fifteen feet away I threw a rock ahead of him and he got straight up pointed the gun took a big draw then just came up and cut his throat so fast that he was in shock. As he looked at me I could see the life running out of his body as he slowly fell to the ground and started to shake, and that was it for him.

I had to get back to the barn because that's the last place that these guys are going to look for me. They were out on the trails and searching the woods. As I left and headed back up the trail towards the barn my heart was still in my mouth and pounding harder than it ever has. I could see the barn in the distance. I started to run as fast as I ever did to get there before the others got wise and came back looking for me. As I got closer I could feel the presents of someone watching so I stopped dead and fell to the ground close to the edge of the trail. I just sat there for a few minutes looking around trying to see through the darkness. I saw movement about twenty feet from the barn in the middle of an old tree. At first I was not sure but after taking better cover I watched the tree more carefully, just then I could see the outline of a man with a shot gun, he was about fifty feet from where I was standing, now, how am I going to kill this prick? I had no time to lose. I took off my socks put a big rock in each one, took the last of my line it was about thirty feet long. I tied a sock on each end stepped out of the darkness on to the open trail and then I started to use this weapon like a bolo. The poor guy did not know what hit him. The line got him right across the mid-section and squeezed the life right out of him. While attaching him to big branch that he was hiding behind, I ran up to get his gun. I looked up at him tied to the branch my eyes started to focus on his body, the line almost cut him in half. As I looked at his face his head was huge and was getting bigger, as I started to run for the barn he popped and all his insides fell to the ground. I had to get a better look while I had time; I was amazed when I entered very slowly. There were two very large tunnels that were lit up like a baseball field. As I went further inside this place I got very scared. I never felt anything like it. I had to leave this place right now. Something's very wrong and if I learned anything doing what I do is to listen to your instincts. Just as I started to head for the door I could hear voices outside the barn, and there were at least five that I could hear, but who knows how many are out. I ran inside one of the tunnels I was amazed how big these tunnels were. You could drive a box truck through very easily. My plan was to run and hide, but there was no place to go, so I turned back and started to run as fast as I could while yelling for help. I could hear the others coming to my rescue; it was crucial that I remained cool headed. As the first 4x4 came tearing up the tunnel looking for me, I was acting like I just came from the other side, I started to tell the two guys that were on the bike that he took me by surprise and took the 4x4 the guy that was driving the bike got on his two way radio and said we have more wounded. With that short call there were more bikes coming, this guy peeled away chasing the guy that was not even there, meanwhile the others were coming to help me thinking that I was one of them. The first bike zoomed right by me then another, then came one more, this one stopped for me, "are you allright"I replied," yeah, just a little dizzy,

" Get on, I'll take you back", I had to think fast, he wants me to go back to a place that I have never been, and if that happens the jig is up it's only a matter of time before they realize that there was no one else in the tunnels, so I told this guy to take me to the barn. He was more than happy to help me, "I hear you man lets go." I got on the back of the bike, and this guy wouldn't stop talking. "Your new" he kept saying," I don't recognize you, what chapter are you with? Because I have been here along time and this is the first time I have laid eyes on you. What's the score?" So then I got angry and said "just drive and shut up, your making my head spin!" then he would not stop talking, he was asking me. "What did this guy look like? What was he wearing?" I swear this guy was on speed. As we approached the barn there were two others waiting with others on the way. As I got off the bike one guy said" welcome to Canada my U.S. brother, we have big trouble, we have to make a clean up before daylight". I agreed fully saying" lets do it but first I need some air, hay! My friend take me for some air before we clean up", done my brother lets ride. As we got on he 4x4 I could see other bikes coming and a lot of them. As I looked at this endless stream of lights coming from the hills, my gut was doing back flips. As they got closer you could feel the earth vibrating under my feet from the rumbling of the Harleys. This was not a good sign, they're looking for me and I am the only one who knows it.

My nerves shot. I can feel my hands starting to shake as they get closer, so I tell my new friend to take me for my air. As we mount up on the 4x4 his buddy calls out "wait." With time running out I acted fast, I cut my rides throat then pushed him off the bike then took off as fast as the bike would go. I had to get the cop's attention so they would look, if these guys catch me I am toast, there's no way I can take all of them but there's one thing for sure I have to disappear for awhile, and let things cool down.

While I'm planning my next job and this job will be my biggest yet, I thank God everyday and then ask for forgiveness and the strength to do my next job safely and to guide my hands as I take so much life into them. As I was returning to move my truck to head home the roads were full of bikers and police it looked like a war zone, there were hundreds of bikers pulled over to both sides of the road with at least the same amount of police. The cops have no idea what just happened less than a mile away, and the bikers never arrived because of the police pulling them over before they got to where I was. It was a good thing that the cops were there at that time or that night would have changed everything. I bought me enough time to leave the scene safely, again without being seen at all. I do a lot of thinking between jobs especially when I'm driving alone. All that has happened that night will return to haunt me. While I drive home to get away from my work it will follow me forever, waking me up at night or while I'm stopped at a red light and the red light becomes one of my victims as it replays over and over until the sound of the horn of the person waiting behind me at the light or when I'm sitting down to eat, or should I say try to eat. One day I sat down to eat pasta and as I looked at my plate I seen one of my victims on the plate that I put through the wood chipper. Needless to say, I don't eat much pasta anymore, or anything for that matter. My diet consist of mostly meal replacements without that I would surely die from starvation, but that's all part of having such a strange (job). Every time I do these jobs I feel that it takes part of my soul.

After this last job I had thoughts of stopping all together. I hear the news on any given day about bikers killing themselves and causing havoc among the upper ranks, and all the raids that has happened because of me, all the money I took and buried or distroyed. These guys or the police still have no clue who I am, that's all the police know is that I am on their side, and the bikers know that there is a vigilante so this will make it harder to do my job

but not impossible.

After I return to my little farm and my wife and my real life for a few days I knew that the peace that I felt there was not to last, but thankful to have it. Every moment. It was time to go back to work I took all the info: I gathered at the bikers farm and it was incredible these guys took four farms, two on the U.S. side and two on the Canadian side, and the only thing that they were doing was they had cut tunnels directly through the mountain connecting the two sides. The entrances were disguised as barns built right into the hillside, and the other two farms that were next to them had the same tunnels, but they were growing weed under ground, it was just like a industrial hydroponics growing operation. The dope they were growing they were shipping it all in a safe place that would probably never be found, if it were not for me! So I made a crude map and a small note saying, "The bikers own the farms" in the map, and" the dope is in the mountain", signed. The Handyman. The police had to act fast because the bikers are still cleaning up my last mess and they know it was me. Later that afternoon the police and the F.B.I. and other branches of the law made a raid on the farms, they hit the jack pot they got tons of coke and over a million pot plants growing in the tunnels, plus cash, Millions of dollars. They were amazed at how the bikers took a farm and turned it into a smuggling operation. The other tunnel was a direct route from Canada to the U.S. from one farm to another. The bikers were really pissed; this was a major blow to the bikers and everyone that they deal with. This was the straw that broke the bikers back, and now they were going crazy, for days after the raid the bikers were cleaning house, there were bodies found every day most of them were torched before they were killed, this shows me that they are still scared and they still don't know anything about me at all, and that's a good thing. Now they must think that the Handyman is a rouge biker or something. The last biker the police found was hanging from a tree by his arms and he had no bottom half. The police said he was put through a wood chipper feet first most likely to make him talk. This resume shit was coming common practice with the biker, and the police loved it, well the press that was a different, they could not get enough of the Handyman and all his gains in the fight against organized crime. There were a lot of positive press, and the public was like hungry fish. The minute the paper or the news started anything about the Handyman the people loved just loved it, they would buy anything with the Handyman written on it. Everytime I do a job the newspapers go right through the roof, I have become somewhat of a folk hero even though know one has ever seen me. All the kids want to be, just like Batman. But I am real and the kids know it and are thriving to achieve goodness instead of evil. When I heard that it makes it all worthwhile.

I guess it's back to work with all the damage I have done with my last job, I almost had trouble to find work, but then without warning there was an attack on a reporter that was a big fan of the Handyman. The day before this attack there was a big writes up in her column on all the good work I have done and if you add it up in terms of money it's in the billions and that hurts, it pretty much crippled the bikers. I guess the bikers don't like bad press so I decided to have a talk with this reporter about month after, but before that I went looking for the bikers that shot her. It doesn't take long to hire a hit man when your company is broke. The bikers were hungry for money so they were taking anything that came along. So I played that card, left a deposit at a known biker bar so I would get a bite, telling the barmaid I need a hit man to kill my wife, of course I was in disguise and I used a summer home of one of my customers as a place to use. Within 24 hours I had a bite. As I entered the bar the barmaid approached me and guided me towards a table with a gang of four bikers, two that I knew and two I did not. As we approached the table one of the bikers had to leave. This guy must have been the hit man, because the others had nothing to hide. The Hit man did not want me to see his face that's why he left. As I sat down with the others there was no time to waste at all, one of the bikers that I knew said "twenty and no deals, cash and a photo, you bring it hear and leave it with Screws."

"How do I know that you won't rip me off?" I said,

" You don't. How do I know that you're not a co?" he said."

" I will give you half down half when it's done, I am not going to be ripped off that's a lot of money to give someone you don't know," he said" what's the matter you don't trust us? Don't we look like people you can trust?" Then he started to laugh and so did the others. It was funny in a sick way with the three of them sitting there in a sleazy bar in biker dress and showing their colors saying trust us. Anyway they agreed to the terms, which kind of surprised me, but showed just how desperate they were. I told them that I would be back tomorrow-same time with the money and the photo, now I had to put plan into action. I got everything ready at the house, I planted my .22 in the living room under the drapes then I put my fish knife in the big chair in the hall plus I had some knitting needles placed above each door frame just in case.

I headed back to the bar with the photo, (someone's grad picture) plus the address of the house where I planned this whole thing. They told me within twenty hours of the down payment.

So I went and dropped off the money with Screws, then headed back to the house to wait for my friends. I wanted this to be just right, so I dressed up like a woman so I would attract them a little easier

because they are yellow, unless there are a lot of them. One on one is unheard of with the Bikers. I am counting on four of them showing up so I will be ready for anything. Not long after getting ready they showed up just like I planed. Two went around the back and the other two came to the front door. I was inside with my blood pumping as fast as ever. They were banging on the front door but I just ignored it. Then the back door opened very slowly the creek was just an alarm; I went quickly through the house grabbing my fish knife on my way. With my dress flowing I ran passed the door so the two guys at the back would see me. Then they gave chase, yelling all the way" she's here she's here", but the front door was locked tight. The others were trying to break the door down. I was hiding behind the bedroom door while one of the Bikers that were chasing me broke off and was trying to open the front door, but the other was in the room with me "yelling where are you? Your husband wants you dead bitch and I'm going to help.

Where are you? Have something for you baby" I was itching to take him out, but timing was everything. As he kept yelling, "come to papa baby" I could hear them talking down stairs. The guy inside was telling them to go around the back, just then I pushed the door slowly so I could see him. He was just getting ready to look under the bed when I said Hi! Papa, he looked up at me and before he could say anything my knife was in his ear up to the handle, as his body fell to the floor shaking like he was having some kind of fit. The noise drew attention to the guy downstairs, he yelled up "did you get her, hey when there was no answer on the second yell panic set in. He started to yell for his two friends, TROUBLE, then all hell broke lose. The three men started up the stairs I was just hiding beside the top of the stairs in a hall closet with no weapon at all. I left my knife in his head, to limit the mess that I would have to clean afterwards. I could still hear his body shaking on the floor and so did his friends. Heard one of them say he's o.k. He's fucking the bitch. Listen he's in the room with her and that's just what it sounded like as his body was shaking on the floor. Then he stopped and that's when the lead Biker said: you go get the bag out of the car, as that one left the other one was yelling" come on lets go we're burning daylight, speaking to the guy in the room, then as they were walking to the room I crept down the stairs into the living room and got my .22 from behind the drapes, then I heard the guy upstairs yell" OH FUCK" he saw his buddy. Now the two of them came down the stairs two at a time running as fast as their feet would carry them, but when I stepped out from the living room with my .22 and a plastic bottle taped to the end of it the look on their faces was priceless, but it wasn't the gun that they seen first it was me standing there6ft2inch with a full beard and a red wig and wearing a powder blue full length granny dress. The look was just like seeing a deer in the headlights, before they could react I aimed and fired one each poof, poof. The first guy I got in the left eye and fell right off onto his face. The other one I got as he turned to run back up the stairs. I got him center right in the back of the head, he to fell on the stairs but there was still the guy that went for the bag. As I was getting ready to finish the two guys in the stairs, the other came running in from outside, "lets go, there's a cop running our plate." Then he saw me standing there in my blue dress, he was speechless and did not know whether to run or scream, but when he saw his buddies he screamed so I pop him right in the face poof, poof. Two shots before his body hit the floor. Now I had to work fast, the police were running the plate of their car, then they just left very slowly just like they came, I took the four bodies and put them in the trunk of the same car that they came in and waited for darkness the drove the car to the post where the reporter was shot, and I left her a message on her service saying this "This is the Handyman there is a gift in the caddy's trunk, your attackers, if you speak to the police you didn't hear it from me, or there will be no further contact". She said nothing to anyone. The police found the car after someone else saw blood dripping from the trunk and reported it, so now I have a good contact I hope, I will test her again before we make first contact just to be sure. After the police found the bodies and a little note from the Handyman saying this "Here is the trash that shot the reporter", signed The Handyman. With this the police went and asked for a positive I.D. from the reporter and with out doubt she I.D. them.

The very next day in her column she wrote a piece that personally thanking the Handyman for his fast work in catching the bikers that were responsible for the worse kind of crime, and that is (attacks on women). And the rest of the crooks and killers let this be a warning to all of you the Handyman is out there and he seems to be everywhere and no one knows who he is or what he looks like so take this warning and beware or the Handyman will get you, so be good people. Then with in a day or two of her column the bikers started all over, trying to figure out who I was. By killing their own this was a big mistake, because it is starting a mutiny among the ranks. You can't trust anyone they are killing each other at an alarming rate and if it keeps up, there will be no more Bikers. It is getting to the point where the Bikers are calling the Police, because they are scared that the Handyman would get them.

It was reported that the Police were called to a small apartment in the east end of the city, where two members of an un-named Biker gang was held up. They had called the Police asking for help because they feared that the Handyman was watching them. This did not amuse the Police, and when they asked the Bikers what the Handyman looked like, they could not answer out of fear. When the papers heard about this is was like a feeding frenzy. They headed right for the holding cell where the two Bikers were. They refused to talk to anyone", I just wanted to go to jail", they both replied! To the Judge they went on, with a list of things that they have done, trying to increase their time inside. The Judge in this case was a closet fan of The Handyman. Every time it had something to do with the Bikers turning themselves in for the same reason, he gave a light sentence to get them back outside. They did this so they wouldn't use the Jails as a safe house. With these two guys he granted them freedom instead of jail, playing on their fear and it worked. The two Bikers freaked out in the courtroom yelling" it's my right to go to jail" then started punching people, and grabbed a gun from a security guard. He started to shoot randomly in all directions saying "kill me"everytime he fired. His buddy started to scream" kill me" so he did and then took his own life. The Judge was given sometime off for making such a bad call. The newspapers loved it; here is two guys that terrorized people for God knows how long. The Judge gave them what they deserved and the people agreed. The Lawyers for the Bikers won't say anything. They just say guilty like a legal aid lawyer, they are to have fear of The Handyman. After all the dust settled, the streets had an eerie quiet to it. It was unsettling to see nothing or no one on the streets after a certain hour, but it was a good thing it was so quiet. You could hear a pin drop, and my little blond reporter was very happy of this. Saying in her next column" I think that the peace that I feel is very comfortable, and the quiet is a welcome site. I would like to thank the Handyman for all he has done for us in this city. If it was not for him the city would be in chaos, the Police try their best but are limited to what they can do. They have to follow the law and that is very frustrating for most of the Police involved. I just want to say Thank-you Handyman whoever you are. I support you along with the public".

Within days of Jessica Mullins writing this, I had an incredible urge to meet this reporter. I knew where she ate, where she lived and where she worked. It was almost impossible to get close to her. She always has two or three people with her, so I had to meet her publicly. I just want to meet her in person to get a feel of who she is, and if I want to use her as a contact. I had to be sure of this before I gave her any information concerning the Handyman. I tried more than once to meet her casually, but there was just to many people. At one point we made eye contact and I felt the strangest thing from her. We did not meet, but not long after I left these places trying to meet Miss Mullins. I decided to go home to my Farm to catch up on my own work, and not to draw suspicion to my wife. After all I am suppose to be working, so I put a little paint on my face and hands and returned home to the Farm. After all the small talk between my wife, and me she brought something to my attention that kind of bothered me. She said" from now on you have to carry a cell phone so that I can reach you. Sometimes I get scared when your not here", then I said" you have nothing to worry about. Look around you, you're on a Farm with your brother and I am here now. The crime is at its lowest in years, don't you read the papers? She started to feel a little better". Then we went on like normal, I did my chores and she did hers. Then there was a radio broadcast announcing a blood drive at a local school. One of the celebrities is (guess who) that's right Jessica Mullins. So I decided to go to donate my blood just so I could meet her. Then I would know for sure if I could trust her or not. I am a big believer in first impressions. I headed down there after waiting for hours and meeting most of the celebrities; it was my turn to give blood. The moment I sat down and they hooked me up, this young blond woman sat in the chair next to me. She asked me "do you come often?" 'Joking', I started to answer her when our eyes met. It was something I have only experienced one time before and that was when I met my wife. It was love at first sight. This was impossible I am married. I can't think that way, so I tried to shake it off and continue a conversation. Between her and me I don't think we said five words. We just stared at each other like dummies, then she introduced herself and apologized for staring. My name is Jessica Mullins. Do I know you? No I don't think so, my name is Garrett Berryman. I'm here just to give blood and do my part. I asked her if she was the same Jessica Mullins that writes for the papers? Yes she replied! Are you a fan?, yes a big fan I replied, then she asked me something that I was not expecting; What do you do for a living ,Garrett said I'm just a Handyman. Then after catching that, I went on to say a Painter, Artist, and Farmer.

Then the nurse said it's over and it was time for me to leave. So I said good-bye to Jessica. It was nice to meet you I said. She answered me; it was a pleasure to meet you, too. Then she said are you doing any work in my area? Because I'm in need of a Handyman, can you help? I said sure and gave her my home number. I was very clear that she should leave word with my wife if I am not there. She replied; I will do that. How busy are you? I'll make time for you I said with a smile. She went bright red, blushing uncontrollably. Then she said, we must have met in another life, because I feel that we have this karma or something. I feel the same thing, isn't that weird? Very she said. I never question my feelings when it comes to first impressions. By telling me that we will become friends. I agreed fully, and then extended my hand in friendship. Before saying good-bye she grabbed my hand and looked at it and said you must work very hard, your hands are so big and rough, but you have such a kindness about you. I look forward to working with you and I will call. Good-bye for now, or should I say see you later. Then she gave me a look that could have melted steel. I don't know if it was intentional but it stuck in my mind like nothing I have ever experienced. All I could think about was this young girl about half my age. I have never been so distracted by someone; it's very unsettling to say the least.

As time passed my life became almost normal. I was doing real work with my hands, creating things instead of destroying them. It was not to last because crime doesn't sleep. The next day there was a News report, and it was talking about a woman that was found half beaten to death. She was in serious condition in the Hospital. The Police say that her ex-husband is responsible and is being sought by Police. Then they gave his description and showed a photo. I recognized him right off the bat. It was one of these Pedophiles that were involved with the Club. This guy was small time

And I did not take care of business like I should have. I was out for bigger fish. Given time, all the small fish get bigger, because the bigger fish are gone. It's time to pay a visit to my friend. He has a very bad habit and I know what it is, (little boys) and I know just the place where he might go, but there is one thing that concerns me. Did this woman have kids? I will bet any money that she has at least one boy. Now I have to tell my wife that I'll be gone for a few days, while I look for the freak. This was not as easy as I expected. Most of the criminals are gone under ground and are not visible as they once were because of my handy work, but it's better that way, I would much rather have to look for it than to have it in my face. That's a sign that you have to fight fire with fire to get results, and I got results. The police have me and without me no results.

Anyway after looking for the freak for a day or two, I hit paydirt. I had seen our friend going to visit another Pedophile that I seen at the same club as the rest of the freaks. I have him on file just like the rest of my surveillance victims I found by watching this one club that catered to pedophiles, now the question is, how do I handle this? He did not kill anyone, (or he might have), because at first he was a woman beater, now he's a woman beating pedophile but the cops don't know that about our friend, and I do. By the time they find anything out I will give our friend to Jessica Mullins and test her as my contact all at once. It is very important if I am to continue my work as The Handyman to find a trustworthy contact, because I can't trust the police just yet. So I started to watch this guy and the things I seen this guy was making me hate him with every hour that I sat there. I had to finish this job fast. This guy was a real problem and from what I seen it looks like he has a mental problem. Every time he leaves the house he is pulling this young boy into his friends van, then they go to a crack house, after about fifteen minutes they came out. This time the boy was crying and very upset (that's not good) for him. I quickly ran towards him as fast as a train moving at top speed before he could even turn and see what that noise was. I was on him like water on a sponge. He didn't know what hit him; the boy was screaming like crazy, our friend was out cold and bleeding from his head. I through him in the back of his friends van and was telling the boy that I was a good guy, I work with the police and were going to get help. He calmed down a little but was still crying a lot.

Our friend was starting to come around and was groaning took this guy and the boy out to a building development site, where I knew we would not be disturbed. I took the freak from the van and told the boy to stay there, the boy just sat there sobbing. This is what I enjoy. The punishment part, not the killing, so I started to talk to the freak," do you know who I am"?"

" No, who are you? And what did I do to you"?

" It's not me" I replied." It's your wife that you beat, I am

The Handyman and you are a threat to all mankind, you are a freak and I am going to teach you how to be a victim." I started to beat him making every punch count. I could feel the bones breaking with every blow, he kept passing out and that did not discourage me, it just gave me better aim. I made sure when he wakes up he will pray to die. After I was finish with the freak I put him back in the van covered him up and drove him and the boy back to a house of the other freak, then I told the boy to stay while I call for help. He just looked and nodded, and then I made the call to Jessica Mullins. She answered; so I gave my speech," Hi, I am The Handyman just listen or I will hang up. I need a contact and I trust you, if you fuck me I'll find another contact."

" How do I know you are the real Handyman?"

" Here's your first tip." I told her about the van and the guy that the police were looking for were inside along with a boy that was being abused, and the van belongs to another Pedophile and that they should check his apartment at the same time, she was marking everything down, then she thanked me and said "I have to work very fast before I call the police, and she did. She went right to the seen opened the van saved the boy and called the police. After they arrived on the seen it was a mad house, they arrested his friend. His apartment was full of child porn and lots of evidence for the police to use.

The next day Jessica wrote about her experience and thanked The Handyman for his fast service in catching this criminal that will most likely (after receiving this beating) think twice about it again." The boy is fine just upset; you must have got there before they had a chance to abuse the boy

and that's a bonus. It turns out that the boy was a son of the woman that he beat and she will make a full recovery. I am not sure about our friend, he will suffer the rest of his life with some kind of pain with all the bones you broke, but that will act as a constant reminder to him as he ages. If the police had got him first he would most probably be walking around waiting for a court date. Thanks for being first and thanks for the tip I will gladly accept any others that you give me, and if I can help you in anyway contact me, you have my number. I don't know how you got it but feel free to use it again at anytime. I will never reveal my source of information so your I.D. will be safe with me, thanks again from the victims and myself and all the police that root for you under there breath, until the next time J.M."

This was a very clear message to me. She let me know how everyone was, and the condition of the freak by writing in her column knowing that I would read it and telling me she can be trusted and I believe her, and from now on she will be my contact, my only contact. I wouldn't ever call the police anymore it's to risky and the more work I do the more popular I get so it is getting harder to do my work without being seen. The crime has gone down big time, but it never goes away there's always one asshole that thinks their smarter then everyone else. I went back home where the Handyman was the talk of the house, my wife very excited about the fact that the Handyman took the time to catch this guy even though he was not a major crime figure. It shows that he is a caring person, he should have killed him but he didn't, he wanted the guy to pay by the law for his crime along with the beating, and that's what they need a good beating. The police can't do that but that's what they need, I would like to shake his hand. This was very unusual, for my wife to be so excited about this kind of thing. She was always a fan of The Handyman, but this job made her happy for some reason. As she went on and on how happy she was I had to ask her "Why are you so happy about this? You never cheered before for this guy, why now?"

"Because if I could I would give my sister's name to the Handyman and tell him to beat Gary my sister's boyfriend, just like he did to the guy in the paper because he beats her to, but I have to mind my business because of the kids, but one day he will get his for sure."

" What goes around comes around." I said. I took this information and thought about doing something myself, but that would mean for me to travel out of province and that's to long for now, but maybe a good scare would work, or better still lots of people looking I called Jessica Mullins and said this! "It's me The Handyman just listen, there's a guy beating his wife in Winnipeg that needs a lot of attention put on him, or I will go down there and he must know that. If you write about this guy maybe he'll go away". I gave his name and address and his wife's name and then hung up. The next day in the Paper she wrote: "We have a problem we will call it a

O.o.p. s that's short for (out of Province situation), The Handyman has informed me that there's a man beating his wife in Winnipeg but his wife is too afraid to speak up so we have to support her with a lot of attention so she knows she's not alone. Her name is Lindsay Davenport." and she gave the address, boy oh boy, the next day when the paper hit the news stands there were people camped out on Lindsay's front lawn, and I'm not talking five or six, I'm talking hundreds of people and police and the media, it was all over for Gary. The jig was up, he went outside to an angry mob almost everyone was carrying a sign that said Woman Beater, or Scum. One guy that was there was huge, close to seven feet tall and he had a sign that read come get some, "give him to The Handyman" said another sign with an old lady shaking it up and down, all this was on the news. Gary had to leave and he was arrested and charged for beating his wife, but the best thing was Lindsay met a lot of good people from her front lawn that stayed camped outside for weeks to make her feel safe. I don't Gary will beet anyone soon, his face was everywhere for a while.

I called Jessica and thanked her for doing such a good job and she asked me "When will I meet you?" I replied "not yet." then hung up. There's nothing I want more is to meet this girl again, but I don't think it's a good idea because I have a thing for her and it will turn into something when we meet again I can feel it. I never felt this way before for anyone, and that look she gave me is stuck in my mind, that look meant she felt the same about me as me, not The Handyman and that's a good thing that's why I trust her. The feelings I have are hard to ignore. They are animalistic just like the uncontrollable urge I have to be The Handyman, I can't explain it but I feel I must act, the drive is tribul my heart beating like a tribe going to war, it's like I have the drum in my chest and I can hear it in my head beating slow at first then, slowly it would get faster and faster until it is all over, in most cases it's like I am watching myself from the outside looking in, maybe that's why I don't feel guilt. A small part of me knows that it's wrong but a bigger part of me says it's right, after all if I don't do this who will? No one that's who, that's why I must do what I am doing otherwise the crime would be out of control.

After returning home my wife was freaking out "where have you been"

" Working" I replied,

"Yes I know that, but you should have called, have you seen the news at all"

" No" I said

" Lindsay's all over the news, and I must go down there, there's people on her lawn, Gary's gone he left in a hurry and I don't think he'll be back", then she went on to tell what happened, and as always I pretended not to know anything. I gave her money and told her to be careful. After my wife left for her trip, I decided my work as The Handyman had to slow down some, so I could take care of my farm and my real business, but as usual it never works out that way, my phone never stopped with people calling me to work and I had to take it to maintain my real life outside The Handyman, but crime doesn't sleep or take a vacation. I was working twice as hard as I normally would. After catching up with most of my chores and pleasing most of my client's, I got the one phone call that scared me the most, and I knew who it was before I answered it. It rang and rang then I answered it. "Hello stranger" she said, it was Jessica, I replied "Hello", then she asked me if I time for her, I said" for you I will make time", she giggled, then thanked me, left me her number and told me it was to do some work like painting and small repairs, the sooner the better, she said, I take my vacation this week if you could do it then, I agreed fully, I told her I will be there Monday morning, she was thrilled "I'll see you then" she said. Before that day would come I would have to do another job as The Handyman but little did I know how this job would change the scope of things to come, it was while I was watching the Pedophiles, I had this guy on file but like other small fries, I did nothing since the last one I am looking back on some to make sure that they don't offend or abuse other kids, that's when I seen something out of the weird. Besides the regular shit this guy was Arab or something along those lines, and he worked a normal job as a lab Tec at Biochem. Every second night he would go back to the lab for sex with the guard, nothing fancy he would suck off the guard and the guard would let him in a restricted area, then what ever he took he would bring it back it to a office the same night, the office belonged to another Arab looking man, this was very strange, what was so important that he would have to suck a dick to get it? And it wasn't very big it was in an envelope. Before I do anything I better be careful he works at a lab, guns I can deal with, germs are a whole different ball game. That was my first hunch. He's selling germs to this guy in the office, I think I'll look a little deeper, so I went back to the little Arab's house and found a lot of different things that made this guy very weird, and I also found what I was fearing the most, envelopes in the fridge most were marked in Arabic, so I took pictures of every piece and left this place just the way I found it. Then I headed back to my place to have a look at what I found. The next day when I started to translate from the Internet, it was not good. I had to be sure before I caused a panic. Among the photos I took were some of a book that went into details of a terrorist attack on all the major cities, there would be no big bomb blast, just a simple brown bag in the tunnels of the whole metros system, after the train hits it's the dust that carries it will contain small pox's and will infect millions of people. This is the worse news that I could have run across. There were no dates on any of the papers, so this may have already begun, so I must work super fast. This guy was not selling the germs just showing the buyer. The little Arab was a major player, if a leader with all that shit he had in the fridge maybe he's the supplier. I must confirm that facts first before

I contact the right people. So I made a call to Jessica "Listen carefully, I might be on to something very big. But before I go in I must confirm the facts first and if I am right this could save millions, I will leave you some photo's to look at, I want translations on the Arabic, can you help me?"

" Yes!" she replied. I rushed the photo's over to her via a pastor I trust that owed me one. When I called back she was very upset and a loss of words, she was insistent that we contact the proper authorities," I will when I find the rest of the cell. I am sure that he is the head of a terrorist cell

that has no clue that I know anything, so far I know of two, him and a very rich Arab. I will watch for a time of two days, if I don't find anything I will give you the O.K. to tell whoever you have to. The more I find the longer we wait," she agreed.

In the first 24 hrs I found the phone that he was using and two others, one of Arabic descent and the other was a white female that was married to the Arab, (or Brain washed). Anyway she was involved big time. I think it's time for me to do something. I have to be careful not to cause a panic but to prevent one. So I called J.M. and told her the shit was going to hit the fan, and she was to be ready to act, she contacted the authorities and filled them in, now they were waiting for me, if they get involved right away it might jeopardized everything. The authorities were very impatient. I had to start by getting the first guy with all the stuff in the fridge, then they could get the rest from the phone records and Info from others they arrest I hope.

I went and waited for this guy to leave his house so I could wait for him outside. After about three hours of waiting he finally left, I quickly went up to his apartment to wait for him.

While I was waiting I grabbed all the books and drawings that they have made. They were like manuals on how to release germs through the metro system there were no big explosions just a bag of germs in the tunnels of all the major cities. No one would know that they were infected until it was to late. I just hope that we are in time to stop it. Suddenly I heard the doorknob rattle. I hid as fast as I could in the bathroom. I went in the tub and hid behind the curtain. I heard him entering the apartment I started to get very nervous as I waited for him, and then I heard another voice. A man. Arab speaking, now I was not happy, I just hope the other guy leaves before I had a chance to finish that, I threw the curtain opened sprung out with a frightening yell the other guy screamed, I punched him right in the forehead with everything I had "paff" I heard the bone crack then his body lifted right into the next room landing on my friend he started to scream like a hurt cat. I grabbed him by his head and twisted as fast as I could, the crack sounded like I broke a piece of wood, then he fell to the floor and started to shake and mumbling in Arabic then he died. I got out of there as fast as I could taking all the Info: With me I had to work fast I called Jessica and told her that it was done, I had all the paper work," Why did you take the paper work?" she asked. To make sure that the truth is told through you. If I leave it, they might lie to avoid a panic, if you have copies they can't lie. She agreed. I dropped off the stuff with my homeless friend he gave it to Jessica. After she made copies of everything she made contact with the Authorities. Giving them everything, the address of the Apt where I got everything, they acted super fast. They were very discrete. There were no marked cars at all, they grabbed all the people that were involved and it was a large-scale operation. They were all over the States and Canada and other places that were free and democratic. I sat back and waited for this big announcement, or something so I would know what was going on. I could risk contact with Jessica the law would be watching her big time after this. All I know is that it was big and it was a success. Then it came after about two weeks waiting. It was revealed that they arrested over 125 people and expected to make at least that many more, the plan was like this. At one point the whole World was afraid of Amtrak's so they stocked piled the cure, but that was to throw off the Government. The real threat was Small Pox and there was no big explosion.

Their was Just a brown bag full of germ's placed on the tracks of all major Metro lines in all the big Cities. After the Train hit the bag the dust would travel for days and every time another Train hit, well the same thing would happen. No one would ever know that they were infected until it was too late. Now that's terror, think about it. It would be like passing a cold, and you see how well that works. Jessica was a Hero for uncovering the story and she gave the credit to me. She thanked me in her Column and warned me that the Police are asking a lot of questions. Like who is this person that is watching us? Called The Handyman. So I'll ask the same question who are you and how can we thank you? The people want to know more now than ever. I am getting letters for you not one or two but bags full. Tell me "what to do with them"? And thanks again from your Public and me. Hope to hear from you soon, until next time.

After I read this I had to tone down everything. I went home and started to get back to a normal life. Ha, Ha.It was not long after being back, that I got the call to paint for Jessica. I was like a little boy all over again. I was nervous like crazy and she was the same. She was dropping things and laughing like a little girl the karma was incredible it's like we new each other our whole lives. Even though I was married I felt no guilt about this, and after being with Jessica. That day we had no sex, but it felt like we made love. All day the feeling was amazing and tribul to say the least. The painting was done in a matter of two days. The bond I made with Jessica was a life changing experience. It would change the whole scope on things. Jessica knew I was The Handyman, she told me she knew the day we met at the blood drive. I was speechless but I had to tell her the truth about my work. She was not surprised but encouraging and helpful. Then she asked me "What should I do with this Mail"? I was at loss and overwhelmed by the amount of Mail she had. We made a pack, that she would read the Mail and refer most of it to the Police, because the bulk of it was people asking for help. I am just one man but the Mail seems to think that I am super human. I am not, I cry, I bleed, I hurt. I am just one man trying to make a difference. Now Jessica knows that, and she is the only one that knows anything about me. Going through some of the Mail, she passed me something of interest. Like I think my Husband is The Handyman, and there's a lot of copycat shit happening. The Police were glad to get the tips from Jessica, thinking that she was helping them and was really helping me. That just kept them happy as long as they showed that they were looking. The Mayor felt safer and so did the criminals, at one point the Police announced that they arrested a suspect of being The Handyman. This guy was found lurking at the last location of The Handyman. He was in a Van filled with HiTech listening devices and weapons. He has no I.D. and the Police are trying to get him to co-operate but he refuses to say anything but" I am The Handyman".

The news hit the prison system like a bomb. There were riots everywhere. The Police were called to keep the Peace in more than one prison. The holding cell where they had this guy was evacuated for bomb threats after the third one. They realized it was coming from a cell phone from inside the station, but who? Now the Cop who was making the calls would never be caught after it was announced. It was already too late for this guy who claimed to be something that was not. The Cop who was making the phone calls made one more call from outside the building. He left the phone on, and then went back. After they traced it and killed this poor guy. It just goes to prove my paranoia is justified. When I say don't trust anyone. The Police are not all bad just afew, but they could influence others. Like me leave distrust among the good Cops. It's bad and very tricky to catch these guys and gals of the Police Department, who think the law does not apply to them. To me and my new source Jessica, I think its time for awake up call for the few that are bad. We let them believe they killed The Handyman so I could work with no distractions. If they think I am dead they won't be looking for me. It was not long after they buried this guy (his name was Jon Hammer stein) he lived in a small town and was a nice guy according to his Wife and neighbors. No one knew much about what he said he was doing, just that he was depressed over the last week. Now I must work very fast to catch these bad Cops. I already know of two, this guy and his partner a woman. The both are growing weed in an empty Apt downtown. I know this from my homeless friend who I talk to regularly. This guy is not a bum, he just doesn't want to be found, but is always a wealth of information. I pay him if the tip is good and it always has been good and confidential. I have been using this guy from the beginning always with good results. He told me that the Cops go every day at 11:30 to the Apt and manipulate the Plants. There they're for half an hour or sometimes longer. I thanked him and tried to give him some money and he refused it saying" you have paid me enough. This ones free, there's nothing worse than bad Cops", and I agreed fully, then asked him" to keep his ear to the ground and to stay clear of the Apt the Cops were using". I had to take care of business, how do you call the Cops on Cops? You don't you wait until the time is right then you steal the weed that they treasure so much. That's just what I did. I waited for them to go into the Apt, and I waited and waited almost 90 minutes. How do they do that with no questions asked? There is another involved I'm sure of that, but these two will do. I have to be careful not to let on that it is The Handyman, because I am suppose to be dead. For now that's what I want so I can work freely to find out who killed Jon.

With his death came light. All the bad Cops were starting the same shit and the criminals were in heaven. I decided to let someone else steal the weed. I let my homeless friend tell as many people as he could about the weed, but not to say anything about the Cops growing it. It didn't take long before the weed was stolen. The two Cops were pissed, I was told they had about five pounds dry and over two hundred plants growing and ready to process. This was a big loss for these two Cops. Not long after they restarted the same Lab in another Apt. It was a major source of income for the two of them. The both were upset and I knew that they would have to buy more clones, so I started to watch them for a few days. I was shocked at what I found. The two Cops were full members of the Devils Guards and were a new kind of Biker. They were trained to become Police right from the beginning. Their Parents are full members and there are at least another five Cops that are members from different areas. It's worse than I thought; I first thought it was just a few bad apples. Now it turns out that there are just a few good ones. I have to be careful because once I start back to work all Hell is going to break loose. They still think The Handyman is dead and their being careless because of that. The other criminals are starting their shit to, but the Cops are a big part of it for letting it happen, for a price. Every one of the bad Cops was taking something from someone. With me gone, it looks easy for them, but not for long. After finding out where the Cops were buying the weed, I waited, but taking the weed was not the answer. It just gave me more questions, like if there are that many bad Cops, who is their leader? Is it another Cop or a member of one of the gangs? So far I found seven bad Cops out of nine that I have been watching. The two good Cops are almost ready to retire. I must contact Jessica to let her know to be ready. I told her what was going on and she was very disappointed and distraught, after I told her the names of the bad Cops. One of the names on my list was a friend of hers and she asked me to be extra sure of this female Cop. I told her there was no doubt, I seen her with my own eyes along with her partner growing weed in an apartment downtown. I then told her to do a story on The Handyman, telling the readers that I am not dead, and the Police got the wrong guy. Also telling them that I am coming to get them. I need panic for my plan to work. The next day Jessica wrote a column that read this," Dear readers I have good news The Handyman is alive. The persons who killed Mr.Hammerstein will be caught and there's more, he knows about all the bad Cops. He also knows whom you are, so beware. Criminals The Handyman is back at work. With that column the shit

hit the Fan, the people were at Jessica's work right after the papers hit the stands, asking all kinds of questions. Like how do you know this information about The Handyman? When did he contact you and how and where? She was very tough and refused to answer any questions. Saying to the Police if there's one thing I am sure of it's this" He's going to get all the bad Cops. He told me that in person", and he knows who you all are. Well that's all she had to say. The Police were pissed off that Jessica would not help them. They were saying that it was her duty as a citizen, to help the Police." she said yes your right and I will help the Police. The real Police, not the crooks that claim to be Police. When she told me this, I was glad that she touched a nerve with the Law. It was time for me to go to work. The first Cops were the two that I ripped off. They already had a new Lab set up, with about two hundred plants.

This was a start, so I went to where they were growing the weed and waited inside the Apartment. All I had with me was a can of lighter fluid. I didn't want to take any chances. I filled the Bathroom light bulb full of fluid, and then left quickly, as soon as I could. I gave my homeless friend the Info; to give to Jessica. As it read," The two Cops that are growing the weed will have a fire at approx: 5pm tomorrow when they check their weed at this address", the next day just like clock work the two Cops went to check the weed and Jessica was right there waiting for the fire with her crew of photographer's. She also had her contacts at the R.C.M.P. Then it happened "boom, crash" the windows blew right out of the Apartment. Everyone jumped into action, the R.C.M.P, the reporter Jessica and her crew. Everyone was right there when it blew. I love it when a plan comes together. One of the Cops that were growing the weed got burnt and the other one was arrested. He was charged under the new Anti Biker Law. Now the whole city was a buzz, the Police are Bikers what next? The big question was, how many more are there. Also how high up does it go, if they're not wearing colours to broadcast their membership they look like any one of us? The next day in the paper Jessica wrote her column and had some real good pictures of the Cop on fire, His partner trying to put him out. The column read" Growing weed gets too hot for the Police". Thanks to The Handyman, two Policemen were caught cultivating pot in a downtown Apartment. Turns out that both are members of a criminal Biker Gang and will be charged under the Anti Biker Law. Thanks to our friend that gave us the tip, otherwise no one would have known that these two Cops were Bikers. The Handyman told me, that there is a lot more to come. The City held it's breath, waiting for my next move. It is a very scary feeling knowing the whole City is waiting for me. One man to do the work of the whole Police Department and then some. Everyone either wants me dead or loves me. Everyone wants to know what I look like, but that will never happen as long as I don't talk about my work. No one will ever know who The Handyman really is. Except for Jessica and my homeless friend, I like it that way. A short time after, I was at home doing some much needed work on my Barn. When I got a phone call, my Wife called out to me "the phone" I yelled, "take a message", then she yelled back "it's Jessica Mullins!" in a flash my heart started to beat out of control. It sounded like the same Tribal Drums I felt the first time. By the time I got to the phone my hands were so sweaty I could hardly hold the phone. I was dropping it on the floor and having trouble to pick it up. My Wife asked me "What's wrong with you? She's just a reporter," I know that" then she laughed and walked away. I answered

"Hello", and it seemed like forever before I heard her voice," Hi! this is Jessica", my heart was in my mouth because I said " Hello Jessica how are you?" mumbling like an idiot. She just laughed lightly, then said" maybe if you have some extra time you could come down to my Apartment. I have a lot for me to do. I mean I have something for you to do", then I laughed. It was like we were reading each others mind, I told her" I'll come down the next day". She asked me to come early", so I did just that. I arrived at her place not knowing what to expect. As nervous as I was before, any other job my mind was a mess. I felt that this was going to be a sexual experience and it was driving me nuts. I could not shake that feeling. As I approached her door, my heart was beating at its craziest. It was almost like it wanted out of my chest. Then I knocked she yelled, "Come in"; when I entered the room candles were everywhere. " Close the door and come in" she said, I did just that. As I got further into the Apt my heart became very calm. As if Jessica herself was holding it in her hands. Her voice went right through me like a warm breeze, taking me along for a ride. I had no control at all. Then there she was sitting in front of her computer. The light was surrounding her like she was a flame sending off this very soft glow. It filled the room, she got up from her chair, and the two of us just became one. We held each other so tight that her small frame just melted into mine. She looked me in the eyes and said", your all I thought about when you said you would come". My heart leaped, "I felt the same way", I said, "maybe more". So I picked her up into my arms and carried her into her room. The soft glow of candles filled the room. I placed her down softly on her bed. I then began to kiss her softly around her cheek. Her perfume was driving me insane. As I went further and was starting to open her top, she started to undress me like two great lovers. We kissed and had foreplay for hours, before having any intercourse. It was incredible when it was over. The both of us held each other as if for the first time then fell asleep. We slept all night, and when we woke up early the next morning in the same position as we fell asleep. So close together that air could not pass between us. It was like this incredible force bound our souls, that we could not control.

I was married, but I felt no guilt," how could this happen to me"? This girl is young enough to be my child, but I feel this incredible love for her, and she feels the same way. During our time together she told me she never wanted children so much since she met me, and I felt the same way. I was in my 40's and she was only 26,but it's like we're soul mates. I can't let my emotions get the best of me. I told Jessica" that I had to leave I must continue my work". She kissed me very hard on the mouth to shut me up, and every time I tried to say something she would do the same," please stay I feel so safe with you"." I if I don't leave I might miss something important that I have been watching." I understand she said" sadly as we started to kiss good-bye, the room filled with our Chemistry. It was like someone opened the Hormone gate. Our kissing soon turned into a raging passion. We made love for hours; I never experienced anything like it. I could not get enough of her soft young body. I took over and over to the point that she could not take anymore. She was crying from the sensitivity, but in a good way. After holding each other and not saying a word, I told Jessica" that I have to leave". She had to go to work also. After I left I went to see my homeless friend, who had some interesting information. He told me that there was one Cop that is always in a Strip Club that is run by Bikers. He goes there every Friday after his shift. He could be working under cover, but I doubt it. If I know he's a Cop so do they. I see him in his Patrol Car everyday, so I took the information. That Friday I went to the Strip Club and waited for the Cop to come in. This was a Strip Club in name only. I sat there and ordered a Beer waiting for the Dancers, but there was none. Just a bunch of nude Women walking around talking to the Men. It was very dark and dirty, and then one of the Girls approached me. She looked stoned out of her mind. She asked me "if I wanted to have sex", then went on to give me a price list; it was like she was reading a menu. I just came to see the Girls dance and to have a Beer. If I were going to have sex it would be with you, she just laughed and walked away. Soon after the Cop walked in and sat at a corner table. As time went on the Girls went to him one by one and gave him money. Then he had visitors, two guys. One was a Biker and the other was an old man. They both sat down and were talking for about an hour. The older man got up and went to the toilet, as he passed a table he gave a tap to a guy sitting there. Then that guy got up and followed him into the bathroom. I got up and went inside, at the same time; the two men were talking until I walked in, then silence. I entered a stall and sat down.

After about a minute they started to talk softly. The older guy was a retired Cop. The guy he tapped was the owner of the Bar, a member of a Mob family. This was a case of passing it on; the old guy was the Father of the Cop that I have been watching there, not Bikers, just bad. I think Cops need a lesson in morality. I left the Bar before the Cop did and waited for him outside. About an hour later he came out, he was a little drunk and I knew that. I watched him down five shooters plus the Beer and that was before I left. He was not aware that I was watching him, as soon as he put the Key in the car door I slowly walked up to him. I said," excuse me officer", he turned in surprise. Before he seen my face I had him out cold. I then handcuffed him with his own cuffs and quickly put him in the trunk. Now what do you do with a bad Cop? I just wanted to give him a bad beating, but he's drunk. There would be no point, so I drove his car with him in the trunk to my old friends Farmhouse, where most of my work takes place. I parked the Car in the woods and just waited for him to wake up. The next morning I could hear him moving around inside the trunk, he then must have realized where he was because he started to scream, and then it went quiet. I wanted him to be scared so I left him to think about why he was there. As I got out of the car I slammed the door with force to let him know it's not good. I started to scream at him, all the time I was pounding on the car with a river stone I yelled "What do we do with a bad Cop" BAM, BAM, BAM, on the trunk hood he began to scream out "please don't kill me" BAM, BAM, he was screaming with every pop of the rock, it sounded like gun fire, now I got his attention. "We will have a little talk", I told him who I was and that scared him more then anything else. He knew then he was in real trouble, the bikers would just shoot him, I had other plans. I started to ask him everything and he was more than willing to give me anything or anyone and he was a little reluctant at the beginning, but fear is a great tool. I told him I was going to let him go. I drove his car back to the same spot where I got it from at the club I then called Jessica. I taped all our little talks, and the list of people, judges, cops, bar owners; all these people were members of a secret organization of bad law enforcement. It's where all the bad cops go to get rich, it was organized crime at it's worse, these guys made the bikers look like pussies, they had control of everything there was no safety here. I first thought this cop was just bad by taking pay-off's. But just like the rest of my jobs one thing leads to another, this was big, too big.

Since there was no danger, I contacted Jessica by phone. I did not want my homeless friend involved. I did not want to call Jessica, but she was my only good contact. It was way to dangerous for anyone that was not bad, you don't know who's bad. So this guy in the trunk is about to find out. Like always, Jessica went down to the club where the car was parked took out the tape from the front seat like I told her, then she opened the trunk with the help of the R.C.M.P. and her photographer, well the cops picture was all over the front page, lying in his vomit and with his handcuffs on himself, it was some sight. Along with the pictures was a commentary saying," This is one of many, courtesy of The Handyman." The cop was charged with corruption along with his father who lost his pension. With this new development Jessica was getting threats on her life, but she told me it's all part of the job." I get at least one a day but I can't let that stop me from doing my job or the bad guys win. Right?" she asked. I told her to be extra careful, she said "I will, but I have to see you it's very important", I said o.k. I will call you to set up a time, she was insistent that it be soon", o.k. tomorrow"

I said. I will come to your apartment"

,"No" she said," I am sure I'm being watched, so meet me for breakfast out of town," I agreed I told her I would send my homeless friend with the place. I sent him with a note with the name of a small bed and breakfast just outside of the city, it was all by itself, so if anyone was watching I would know, I was waiting for a long time, I was getting worried. I waited an extra hour and Jessica never showed; now my concern turned to panic. I was trying to keep a cool head but my gut was telling me different. I tried her cell first, no answer, then her work; she did not show up for work. Now I was in panic, I can't just show up and start asking questions. I have to wait. Almost the whole day had passed, my nerves were shot and my hands were tied. I could do nothing but go back to my home. As I entered the back door my wife was standing in front of the T.V. listening intensely, as I said "Hi! I'm back" she shhhhhed me,

"Wait" she said," you know that reporter that you did work for Jessica Mullins," my heart fell,

"Yes, what about her"?

" She's dead," I never felt so sick in my life. My wife just told me that my soul mate just died, my emotions were uncontrollable, I broke down, my wife holding me," what could I do?" she kept asking me "Why are you so upset"? I just told her I was upset because I just met her and she was so young. As the news was released more and more information was released. My sadness turned to anger Jessica was a victim of a drive by shooting, she was found dead in her car on a small stretch of highway just north of the city, she was on her way to see me, I was devastated, I could not even go to the funeral.

No one knew about our affair, or us. It turned out Jessica was pregnant with our child that's what she must have wanted to tell me that was so important. This news was the worst. Now I must find the killers that took the life of Jessica, but before I do I must clear my head so I can think clearly. I started to punch on my punching bag it got to the point where I almost passed out from exertion but I had to keep going, I was on the bag for at least two hours. It seemed like minutes. When

I stopped I had brainstorms, I thought I was having a stroke I could feel the current running across my brain like someone touched my head with two live wires, it was invigorating but scary.

After the event had stopped I went inside to shower and clean myself up, but before I could I went in the living room to get the news and that's when it hit me, traffic cameras. I went down to transport headquarters and gave the person in charge some story about my car being broken into on highway 125 about eight days ago. The person said we have this tape, the police called us and asked us to hold it, and it's very rare that two persons ask for the same tape. I just want to view it, if you give it to the police now, my insurance won't pay, and I'll have to wait for maybe one year. I just want to look if there's anything I can tell the insurance and they can fight with the police. The person understood telling me o.k. I could view the tape but I couldn't take it. I went into the viewing room and started to look at the tape, it was very easy to find and as I watched Jessica's Car come into range of the camera, my heart and my stomach were a mess almost to the point of vomitting. Then it happened a unmarked police car pulled over Jessica, cop got out and began to open fire on the car hitting Jessica with at least five shots, then he got in the car and drove off. There's no way to tell who this cop was, just that it's a cop. I seen enough I returned the tape and thanked the clerk and gave him$50 he was over joyed then I said "you never seen me", he replied! "Seen who". Now I know for sure whom I'm dealing with, it will be a deadly game with no mercy.

I went back to my home and laid low for a month collecting information and putting together a lot of HiTech toys that I collected off other jobs. I went to work I used all the bad money that I saved from the bikers, my funds were unlimited. I had to set up a few cops to get a bite and to see who's bad and who's not. I rented a large warehouse and set up my workshop. I had everything I could think of and some stuff you never heard of. The first thing I did was to rent an apartment, through some fake names and bank accounts so that I could not be traced, then it was time, the first apartment I filled with pot plants and growing equipment and some well placed camera's and listening devices, now I took ten stacks of money $1000 in each stack, each stack had a little surprise took ten musical birthday cards and removed the guts, then placed the guts of each inside the money with a small charge of plastic explosive's and a dye pack of some germs and radio active dust, the germs will act like a cold a bad cold. The dust I'll follow with my equipment and the germ will consume anyone who comes in contact with it, so it will be very easy to keep track of. Then I hacked into the police computers to keep track of who calls in sick. I was all set, I put the bug in my homeless friends hands I told him to put the word out that this apartment is full of weed and money. The person who was renting the apartment is in jail, a biker. I told him a biker because nobody in their right mind would rip off a biker only a bad cop. All the money was in a dresser just sitting there. I put the apartment in the name of one of my victims a biker. I waited for days and nothing, so I made a

911 call from the apartment then left. By the time I got back to the warehouse everything was in full swing. I was watching it just like a movie, I had camera's everywhere. I hid them in the walls so there's no chance of the cops finding them. I was taping everything, and then after it was all over I went over the tapes one by one. I got two suspects already, I

watched one of the patrol cops he seen the money and alerted his partner to it. Before long one of the stacks were gone. I was watching the entry on the P.C.as they entered the evidence, they were one stack short, but it was taken before the detectives arrived. So no one knew it was missing just me and we will soon no who else is involved in this. The money also contained a full dye pack of ink but was not made to explode. This way the cops will think that it was safe to use. Within days they started to call in sick, at least five in 48hrs this is good, the bug will help me a lot, the clock was ticking this bug will only stay in your body for five days, but it's enough time for me. I took my special glasses to look on my money trail, besides who sick? Not everyone will get the bug, but everyone who touches the money, I will know even if it was innocent there will be a trail it glows bright green under my glasses, but is invisible to everyone else. Even my glasses have camera's to record the evidence. The first of five was a fifty five year old man, cop of twelve years. I went to his home where he was sitting on the toilet, like he's being doing for the last twenty-four hours. I entered the house by an open window; he was alone and talking up a storm on the toilet. I took my .22 and sat back in his chair, I made a noise so that he would hear me I could hear the panic in his voice. As the lamp that I just knock over hit the floor. "Who's there"? I heard the splash of his shit hitting the water in the toilet as he kept yelling "Who's there"? Broooom gas fart, then more shit splashed. "I have a gun" he screamed weak and shitting.

I replied! "Me too", then I said" this is for Jessica" and opened the bathroom door he stood up and let go a big wet fart and water, it was all over the top of the toilet and the walls, he just stood there shaking and shitting. I raised my .22 and took aim, he grasped at his chest and fell to the floor, lying there rolling around in pain, then he just stopped, he took a massive heart attack, I didn't even touch him. As I looked around, the money trail was all over his hands and on his persons where he must have been scratching himself. This was my evidence. Now my next sick cop is a family man, so I have to be careful. After I got to his house his wife and kids were all there and sick as well, but he was the man of the house and sooner or later he will have to leave. I cut the phone lines so he or his wife would have to go out. As I sat there and waited for this guy to go out a car pulled up, inside that car was a glow from my dust and the drivers hands had contact also, that must have been where they opened the money. The back seat was lit right up, this is a bonus for me; I can get two birds with one stone (sort of speak). I loaded my crossbow and waited as the cop in the car was looking for something on the front seat, he got out and headed for the front door, he had a plastic bag in his left hand, from what I could see it looked like a drug store bag. I was itching to shoot this guy but I wanted to get the both at the same time (he was unexpected) but on my list also. My mind was racing, how do I kill two guys with a crossbow? Chances are I will only get one shot after all their only cops, then I picked up the crossbow and was taking aim at the front door jus as another cop was knocking, they would have to be close to get the both, then it me, silicone. I quickly grabbed the can and sprayed the arrow. I could hear the cop saying "it's me", I was getting nervous but I work best under that pressure, I took a good aim at the back of the cops head and waited for the door to open, I would only have one shot, then the sick cop came to the door, they started to embrace like friends and I took my shot, thung!! Then it hit like slow motion. As the arrow passed through the both men the look of shock on the cops face as the arrow hit his friend first, he must have seen it, but had no time to react. The same arrow passed through his face under his right eye. I left quickly with no noise; it will give me that time I need to get away.

I got back to the warehouse the news was already on it.

The new crime reporter was a young guy that use to write for a small weekly, he will never replace Jessica, but I will need a contact sooner or later. He wrote a piece on these two cops and said that the arrow passed through both men's heads and went half way through a brick wall behind them, this was a well planed hit and to do it with an arrow, WOW, it turns out that the both cops were infected with the same virus that they found on the last cop that died of a apparent heart attack. "I see a pattern someone's killing Cops," the reporter said. I have to set him straight and I believe in making a good first impression, I contacted my homeless friend and asked him to find out some details on our new reporter, like where he eats, where he lives, is he a drunk or a dope addict. Normally I would do most of it myself, but right now I have my hands full. I must go back and review some surveillance tapes. I went back to the warehouse to review the tapes, with the set up I have I can see in any police station, anywhere there is a camera, it's all run by computers, and I have the best of everything, but what I did not expect was such a large money trail the dust was everywhere, the terrorist sure no how to spread a germ. I learned how to do that through the terrorist I was watching, it was all written down on paper and very easy to follow. Now I have created a monster, the dust has consumed the police; it seems to me like everyone in that one station has been contaminated, I feel that my surveillance has paid off big time.

The bad cops are mostly from the same station. There are two others, they are very sick they must have been in the car with the other three, that's my original five, I killed Three the other two are big shots, so it won't be easy as the other three. I've been very lucky, no blessed up to now. The first thing I had to do was to keep track of who touched the money? While I was doing that, I had an E-Mail from my homeless friend who wanted to meet with some information, I agreed and told him to meet at our usual place, he greed, that was weird and must be important because he never agrees on the first place that I suggest. I left right away, I felt an eerie quiet come over me, and it was very scary. I had my hi-beams on the street lights were on, but still was very dark, as if the dark was eating the light. It was starting to freak me out, after I got at our meeting place I waited just like always, it was not a good night to be out, there was something evil in the air, I could feel it. I could not wait too much longer; I was starting to get paranoid. The longer I waited the darker it became, there was not a soul out not even a car, just me sitting in my van alone in an industrial park, not good. I started the van then bang, bang on my window I jumped back in fright, it was my homeless friend his dirty bloody face was right up against my window, I jumped out to help him he could hardly talk. I quickly put him in my van and returned to my warehouse. He was beaten pretty bad, but would be o.k. After a day or two he got over his biggest wounds and then started to tell me about his ordeal that got him here, over the last month or so some of his buddies just disappeared, he lost at least six other homeless people plus they tried to get me I was lucky I got away alive, they were going to kill me for the fun of it, it was an initiation into a criminal gang, everyone has to make a kill. The cops just pick up the bodies and say it's no big deal and put them in some grave with no name. (They're homeless so it doesn't matter, right.)

I asked him "Why didn't he tell me sooner?" and he just smiled and said "I was trying to make it easier for you my friend", first things first. You asked me about our new reporter he looks to be very quiet, I watched him for three days and on the third day he looked at and said "Tell your friend he can trust me, but he wouldn't know that unless I was given a chance." I was taken back, how did he know? Now what! I didn't know what to say of course, I played like I did not know what he was talking about, but he knows me and if he knows me guess what?"Yeah" I said, who is guy that knows you? Now I have to contact this bird, tell him I said" no" don't give him our meeting place. I don't want you going back there until I clean up first, so arrange a meeting for two days from now at our spot, then I asked, "What's his name again"

" Cory Mullins." I said" any relation to Jessica?" he replied, "a younger brother". I was so caught up in watching the cops; I never even put the two names together. Now we have to meet for sure. Move up the meeting for tomorrow night early around 5p.m. I want you to bring him in person. I'll be waiting. I went back to the warehouse and made copies of all the useable evidence and let my new contact do the rest. The other two are implicated on video along with a gang of others, I am sure once they look at all my tapes, and they will, there will be a lot of heads rolling. The two guys that I got with the arrow, after looking closer at my own surveillance tapes the car that was used to kill Jessica was the same car that the cop came in. Justice was served! And now I feel good about my work again, this was an unexpected bonus that will justify what I do. The cops would have never solved this case without me.

It was almost time to meet Cory Mullins. He was very young just like his sister, and I am not sure how I feel about this meeting. I have some doubts, but I owe it to Jessica to give him a chance, after all she must have spoke of me and my friend, or how else would he know? She must have trusted him a lot or she told him out of fear for her life. I guess I'll find out all my answers when we meet.

I was very jumpy this night, maybe it was anticipation of meeting a new contact or it was something else. I pulled over at the first phone booth and paged my homeless friend and changed the meeting place to a spot along the water not far from the first spot. About two block walk, this way I could make sure he was not followed, but to my surprise what did I find while I was waiting for my friend? But a gang of young men at least 6'5" were eighteen or ninteen, the other was sixteen give or take a year.

They were the guys that were beating up and killing the homeless, that's why I must have felt jumpy earlier, this should be a lesson in what goes around comes around, I took off my socks and put a small river stone the size of a pool ball in each one, then I started to meet my very large brave gang of strong young men and they took the bait, just like a catfish, as soon as they seen me alone they approached me,"hey buddy, do you have any money?"

"Yes, how much do you want?" they started laughing then the leader said "all of it you fool", then I replied to him,

" It's time for me to leave." and I started to walk away, just then the lead guy made his move, he tried to hit me from behind. I grabbed his arm and broke it across my shoulder (snap) right at the elbow, the bone came right out of his coat, the scream sent his friends running, I beat this guy to a pulp, his gang just stayed at a distance screaming at me to stop, I started to taunt them, "Let's go who's next, you bunch of trash"? The guy I just beat was mourning on the ground, everytime he grunted I laid into him. His friends were trying to decide if they could take me, then they all rushed at me as fast as there feet could take them yelling and screaming all the way. I took out my socks and started to spin them, one in each hand, then once they got close enough I let go, one thud hit one right in the face, the other I kept spinning then whack I hit another, then one jumped on my back and the other was throwing punches out of no where (bang, bang)

Then screaming, my homeless friend and the reporter we had them all together, busted and bleeding from all sorts of wounds. My homeless friend and Cory, who was a big part of this whole beating and vigilantism that just took place, to keep them here, I'm going for help. Help meaning a whole bunch of homeless people, we waited for a sign then it happened my friend came back alone and said," you can go now my friends and I will take it from here", I said why don't you take all your friends and your gangsters and your reporter and do it so everyone knows, get the reporter Cory, this is your first story. The homeless fight back, have all the arrest very public call 911 right after, the rest of your friends will arrive and get some pictures, then my Friend said "you must go fast", then Cory said it was a strange experience but a good one." It was nice to meet you, we have to talk another time Cory, I must go my I.D. must remain a secret."

" Your I.D. is safe with me, I am doing this for Jessica" he said, as I was walking away. The meeting went well, I met Cory and gave him his first story and helped my friend feel safe again. Now I have to go back to my home, my wife has a job lined up for me painting and gardening that's a stretch, I think I will enjoy this work for a change. I got back to the house and me and my wife embraced I missed her terriblely, I lifted her up and carried her into our home, all the time she was giggling, "What are you doing "? she asked. I Shhhhhed her and said," Stay here," I turned off all the lights and lit a single candle then took her clothes off piece by piece. With every piece of clothing I took off, I washed her soft warm body with my tongue, kissing and holding, when I got down to her small soft belly button my manhood stood up like never before, I removed her panties and kissed her all over, I turned her over on her belly and caressed her back and neck. As I got down to kiss her lower back, she rose up on her knees. I moved in, I put my penis straight in, she let out a scream, I pulled back and thrusted again then I began to make love. It was intense. I never lasted so long. She was to the point of passing out but I wanted more. I could feel those Tribal drums banging away and that's when I know sex is good because it does not happen every day. My wife was ready for sleep and so was I. We slept for hours holding each other the whole night like spoons.

The next day I felt like a new man, and by the glow on my wife's face she felt the same. Good things don't last forever, it was time to do these small jobs and get back to work. I'm waiting for the paper to see what Cory wrote, and it was a big piece. There were pictures of the entire homeless, turning over broken and bleeding gangsters to the mayor of the city. He was afraid to come out of his office, so his deputy mayor excepted on behalf. It never ends what will really happen to these guys? Not much, they got the worse of it when they got the beating. The rest of the time they will get their three meals a day, a bed and probably all the dope they need. It was time for me to sit down and give Cory the meeting that we never had. I got my friend to get a note to Cory with a map of where we will meet. It will be just Cory and me that will know that location for future meetings. This would be our spot.

It is a small restaurant just north of the city where we could meet safely. Since he already knows what I look like it makes that much easier, I'll still be very careful, trust is earned.

I want to take Cory to my Warehouse, it will depend how I feel after the meeting. I waited about an hour before he showed up. Then another half hour watching him to make sure he was not followed. Then I made contact, I got into his Car and we drove around all over in random directions. We talked about a lot of things. Jessica was our main topic, he kept saying she said, "She met someone and was very happy". For the first time I was happy to hear this. Then he said," she never told me that you were the Handyman", I got that information after she died. She left word with her Lawyer to mail it in case of her death. She must have known that something was up that day. We were bonding like Father and Son. The karma was good. I made my decision to bring him to my Warehouse, but he had to go blindfolded, he agreed fully. I gave him a Black Hood to put on until we arrived. After we entered the Warehouse through the bay doors, they closed behind us and my alarm system detected the extra person through heat sensors, I had to re-

Program it to accept Cory as a temporary visitor. Then I let him out of the Van and removed the Hood. He was in complete silence in what he was seeing. This was Hi Tech in every sense of the word. He was very impressed. He new what a lot of the gadgets were, but was about to be even more impressed when I showed him the surveillance Tapes, of the bad Cops and how deep it runs and how I managed to tap in on Police Video. I showed him the trace Tapes," On the Tapes you can see the money trails with the dust, that I came up with". He was dying to have copies. That could not happen. If anyone knew about the Tapes I would have to abort everything, because everyone would know that they were being watched. This had to be handled with care, Cory asked me," How are we going to work together"? You will never know when I'll make contact, and if I do, it will be only you that will know the location. This place cannot exist to you, the Tapes you seen can never be discussed. If you do, you will compromise everything that I have worked for. The way it is now we can keep an eye on the ones we don't trust, as long as they don't know their being watched. You can never contact me, only through my Homeless Friend and that will take time. I will give you information to help you make your story with the evidence that you could use (trust is earned). He kept going back to the Tapes. I told him again" we can't use them", but I will give you some evidence to stir up some shit. We'll tell the Police that the money was spiked with a germ and anyone who came in contact with the money should contact a Doctor right away, because they could die. That's just what Cory wrote in his Column, he said," I have a new friend he is The Handyman and he tells me that he has a list of bad Cops if you want it. He also said" all the Cops that took that money are going to die if they don't get treated. By that you know who you are. Your friends are dead and as you all are sick it will get you to. I have met this guy they call The Handyman and he is all business. He dislikes Criminals, but hates bad Cops...Beware. He also told me about two bad Judges that took some of the bad money, and showed me Tapes of all persons involved. The money had a Radio Active germ that can only be seen with a certain Lens and a Camera doesn't lie. I am a person that believes with my eyes (hear say) don't cut it. I take my Job seriously, if I wrote it, it's because I believe it". This was a good thing the whole Police Force was in an up roar. No one trusted anyone it was no longer a Police Brotherhood. After the papers hit the newsstands I could see the good Cops they were the guys that were not worried. The others were climbing the walls asking a lot of questions and were suspicious of everyone. Their whole operation was in jeopardy. The panic was very visible in some of their faces. It was like catching a child with their hands in the Cookie Jar. I watched carefully for a few days from my Warehouse making my list and checking it twice before I make my next move. The only way to catch the bad ones is through bad things. You set them up just like the first time, only this time I will give them to Cory. As I sat there making a plan to catch the bad guys, my pager went off. It was my Homeless Friend he wants to meet me it's urgent. I left right away to meet him, all the time thinking what's wrong? Then came the Drums as I came closer to our meeting place, beating like there's no tomorrow. My heart pounding so fast and hard that every time this happens I think is it. As I arrived at the place where he was waiting for me in the open, pulled up and he got in," thanks for coming right away" he said," What's wrong"? I asked," We have a little problem, do you remember our friends in the Park?" Yeah! What about them? The leader was at City Hall wearing a suit paying a visit to the Mayor. That could only mean only one thing. He hired these guys to get rid of the Homeless. Of course it all makes sense now. My next job will be this one; I'll let the Cops sweat it out for a while. I'm sure that they are not going anywhere after that story that Cory wrote. I will get the list of Cops that show up for work. That's easy work; the job with the Mayor is something that Cory will love. Since the Mayor is a bad Mayor. That's all it will take is this story and he's finished, I will gather some evidence for him and get him started. I have bigger Fish to fry. My friend told me about this guy that was always getting drunk and beating his Wife and young Son. He owns a Restaurant in the old part of town. She called the Police once before, but the Cops that responded knew him so they did nothing. She won't call anymore because after they left he beat her even worse and told her that he pays these guys. Nothing will happen to him. She is a prisoner in her own home. That will not do for me, this job is more important than getting the Cops or the Mayor. There's one thing I hate, it is people who think they are above the Law because they have money. Most cases money can buy you your freedom. Not this time, I went to check out the Restaurant it was a Hot Dog joint. This guy was making big money. He opened from5am to 10am for breakfast then he would close and open again at11:30 and close at 2pm.The whole time he is closed, every blind on every Window is closed. You can't see in, a big mistake on his part. I went into the Bathroom just before he was ready to close and hid. I could hear him closing the Blinds and telling his employee's to leave its o.k." I'll see you tomorrow", when the doors locked I could hear him shaking it to make sure it was locked. I put on a Hood and left the Bathroom, he heard the door squeak and said "Who's there", "I said it's me and jumped out in front of him. He screamed and started to yell at the top of his Lungs," Take the money, Take the money", please don't hurt me. I paused for a split second and said I'll show you the same mercy you show your Family. I am not here for money and I started to beat him the anger I felt was pure. There were no Drums; no fast heart beat nothing-just anger. I was throwing him around like a Doll. It was not over he was lying in the corner bleeding from everywhere and he looked up at me and said," When I get her she's dead". I said to him" Some people never learn I think it's because they were not taught. So this is a very important lesson, listen to me never touch you're Family again", then I picked him up over my shoulder and brought him into the Kitchen, he was barely conscious. Took the cover off the hot Grease where they made French Fries, then I shook him to make sure he knew what was going to happen. I took his right Arm and forced it into the hot Oil right up to the Elbow. He was screaming like crazy, and then he passed out. I left him on the Floor; his Arm looked like a big fake Arm all the skin was just falling off.

I removed my Hood and left by the back door. After I left I made a call to Cory to let him know what went on and to tell him to get his Wife out of the house for a few days, and to explain to her what went on before the Cops try to intimidate her. He has Cop friends; so don't tell anyone where she will be. You should be the only one that knows her where abouts, as long as she is safe. If you can't find a place tell me now and I'll run the show." It's O.k." Cory said, "I know all the same people that Jessica knew, she will be fine. Then Cory headed down to the Restaurant while his friends took care of this guys Wife. He got there the same time as the Police; there were no Ambulances, just Police and the Press (care of Cory) and his Newspaper. The first thing he seen was a Policemen vomiting outside the Restaurant. Then the owner came running out, it looked like he had three Arms, as he got closer you could see the skin he was holding in his good hand. It looked like a very soft Arm that was made of Jell-O! And that's the Photo they used. The Camera caught the terror in the face of this Woman beater. That's a wake up call to all men that think they can just blame it on the Booze. This man had money and he knew bad Cops that looked the other way, but didn't help him. So be warned this was the work of The Handyman thanks. I have witness this guy at work, let me tell you the next three stories that you will read will convince you that with out this guy the City would be in deep trouble. He seems to be everywhere, but no one can see him, even his Victims know nothing or don't remember, but what ever works my reader ship tells me that he is popular. As usual my days start some what normal when I am at the farm doing my chores then I receive a phone call it was Cory telling me to watch the 6 o'clock news it was all about the gang wars and the polices refusal to act on immigrant gangs, one officer said we can't touch them because they pay good lawyers they are financed by the music production co, Mostly rap artist and want to be gangsters, So I started throwing underground party's. It brought everyone from the unknown to the very famous, mostly it was regular party goers at first but the more party's I through the word got out. Before I knew it there was famous people showing up.

I was sure to leave reservations for all the well known rappers the whole place was under surveillance mostly the reserved booths were tapped for sound but the whole place was under video watch. We caught a lot of good info over two weekends but the best was yet to come.

Cory was taking reservations for are largest party yet he told me there was people coming from all over the states this is what we have been waiting for. Cory called me and said we need a bigger place. This was a problem but I will talk to my contacts I will come up with something. We don't have much time the party's we were throwing was once a month it was to much to fast. We kept all the big players and gave them reservations. We just could not change are spot. I don't want to jeopardize what we have these guy's and gal's are hard core crime lords we have some of the big time rappers talking about heat seeking missiles and fifty cal, hand guns. We must get as much as we can. We started to put together a list of all the big players and get confirmations on the reservations. Once we get them in the club then we will make some orders. My first orders were heroin, cocaine, ecstasy. and not even a question just how much do you need. The weapons were my real concern. We had offers of fifty cal automatic's stingers you name it. It was all coming from the local base in Quebec. Its now we call in the big guns the good cops had to take over and inform the DEA. It was to much for me. I will stick to my farm for a couple of months, and let things calm down after the upcoming raid